Adventure #2

The Backpack

Craig J. Heimbuch

The characters in this book are fictional, though inspired by real people. Any overt similarity or resemblance to real people is completely accidental and not intended.

For the cousins.
I love you all.

Special thanks to Katie Reeder, a gifted artist with a nifty pizza tattoo, for the incredible cover art. She's got a website on the way and, once it is live, I'll post the address on my Facebook page.

Speaking of which, for more from me, to ask questions or just to talk books, go to http://www.facebook.com/CJHeimbuch

Monster Files Case #13
The Grass Man

Chapter One

Sam hated his new room. It was at the end of the upstairs hallway, above the garage, with a sloped ceiling and blue carpet. The ceiling came to a point in the center of the room, making him feel like he was in some sort of tent or cave. He missed his old room, his old house and his old friends. He hated having to move, to leave his school and his baseball team. He hated it here, he hated this town. Smithville. What kind of name is that for a place?

In Chicago, where they used to live, his room was big and on the third floor, with huge windows that overlooked his favorite park. He had model airplanes hanging from the ceiling, shelves filled with adventure books and scary books and comic books, and a set of Encyclopedia Britannica his grandma gave him for his 10th birthday. He loved that room. His sister, Molly, was not allowed in there and his bed was right under the window. He never needed a nightlight because the streetlights painted the walls a dull orange color. He liked to lie in bed at night and pretend the cars passing outside were enemy patrols. He was hiding deep behind the front, a paratrooper dropped in the wrong place, and he had only his wits and his trusty knife for survival. He played these mind games until he drifted off to sleep. And in the morning, when he woke up, the walls were back to their usual shade of pale blue.

In the summer, he would grab his baseball glove and meet the boys from his class at John F. Kennedy Junior High to play in the park all day. During the school year, he'd walk to the corner with Molly and they would catch the bus to school. He would sit with his friends and trade baseball cards or talk about football. After school, they'd play in the park until dinner. Then he'd do his homework and go to his room, his beloved room, to read about the adventures of Rivers Glenn – the intrepid Geographic Expeditions correspondent, who traveled the world in search of natural wonders, fighting off villains and rescuing victims as he went. When his mom shut the lights off he was back behind enemy lines.

But his new room was dark and there wasn't much traffic on the country road outside. The best he could hope for was that the porch light would reflect off the snow, but the small windows and oddly shaped roof made it hard to pretend. It made it hard to imagine he was anywhere other than in the room over the garage in the country house in this stupid new town.

He missed a lot of things from his old life – getting up early and watching SportsCenter, reading the sports pages and looking forward to Cubs spring training or watching the Bulls on television. But there were no sports teams in Smithville – no spring training, no basketball arena, and no daily newspaper. There was corn – a lot of it – and trees and hills, but other than that, not much. Sam's mom told him the winter might be hard, but when summer comes, she was sure he would have new friends and discover new places to go. When they moved in, she gave him a new Rivers Glenn book and a little light to set on the table next to his bed.

They had been in Smithville for a week. They moved on Christmas Eve and spent Christmas morning unpacking boxes instead of unwrapping presents. They ate pancakes for dinner and drank cans of soda. The television was not hooked up and they all took turns talking to grandma on the phone. It was the worst Christmas ever.

The holiday break had been cold and lonely, and he decided his first day at Smithville Junior High wasn't going to be any better. He was not looking forward to it. He had never been the new kid before, but he remembered how hard the new kids had it back at JFK. Sometimes they were stuffed in their lockers; sometimes they had their books snatched from their arms. The bullies tended to get to them first, to mark their territory like deranged lions. Lunch was the worst – with the bullies slinking like sharks, making their move just as the new kid was about to bite into his hamburger. They put their fingers in the new kid's milk and spit in their cake.

Sam replayed the memories of all the times he had witnessed these atrocities as he was lying in his old bed tragically transported to a terrible new room. He had never been brave. He never needed to be. He did not fall asleep. He tossed and turned, staring at the ceiling, terrified of what the next day would bring.

Chapter Two

Smithville Junior High, like much of the town, was surrounded by cornfields and dense woods. As Sam's mom pulled out of the driveway, leaving him shivering on the sidewalk outside, he began to feel like he had been left on a desert island – a prison, where only the strong survive. Molly, who never seemed to worry about things the way Sam did, bounded straight for the front door to get her schedule and meet her classmates. He wondered how she could be so excited about this, but Molly was the kind of girl who enjoyed homework and going to the dentist. She always got perfect grades and never had a cavity in her life.

Sam stood there looking, staring at the entrance to the school, unable to bring himself to move, to take a step in the direction of his new life. It was all too real, too depressing. He thought about running away, but had no idea where he would go. The bell rang and he knew he should go inside, but he was like a deer standing in the road watching as the headlights of an oncoming car got bigger and bigger. Then he felt a shudder in his back and nearly fell on his face as he was knocked over. He looked up to see what had hit him and caught a glimpse of a red backpack and curly blonde hair as it disappeared into the entrance of the school. Sam picked himself up, dusting off snow and checking his hands for scrapes from the ice-covered sidewalk.

"Are you coming or not?" he heard a voice call from the direction of the door. "You're late."

The woman was old, nearly a hundred in his estimation, with a thick gray sweater covering her pink flowered dress. She was wearing glasses with a silver chain that matched the color of her hair. She stepped outside, her big rubber boots making a thud on the sidewalk, and grabbed him by the arm.

"Young man, this is no way to start the first day of the new term."

Her voice was gravely, like she had broken glass in her throat and she dragged him toward the principal's office. The principal, Mr. Hutson, was waiting for him – and Molly was sitting in an orange chair inside the inner office.

"You must be Sam," Mr. Hutson said, his deep voice booming. He was tall with black curly hair and a wide grin. He smiled at Sam, but he didn't seem friendly. "Please, step into my office and we'll get you all set up for your first day."

After a brief introduction to the school rules and policies, Sam was lead by a student aide to his first class. Mr. Hutson said the aide's name was Adam – and Adam did not say a word, just walked quickly, five steps in front of Sam, down a long corridor with big windows overlooking a courtyard. Adam stopped in front of a door and pointed, grunted something and walked passed Sam, who thanked him for the directions.

Sam's shoes squeaked as he neared the door and he opened it to find a ghastly sight. On top of the tall, long, black science desks sat pig heads, one for every two students. Their tongues were hanging out and their eyes were glazed over. In the front of the room, a short woman with red hair had a pig head of her own sitting on the desk, its skull split open and brain hanging out.

The teacher, which his schedule identified as Mrs. Johnson, peered at Sam through the bottom of her thick glasses and humphed. One of her eyes was much larger than the other, twice as big easily.

"Uh, hi. I'm Sam," was all he could manage to say. "I'm new."

The class giggled and Sam could feel the blood rushing to his face, making his cheeks pink. His stomach began to turn as the smell of chemicals overtook him. He could still hear the kids giggling as the room began to spin and his vision went black. He didn't feel himself fall or hit the ground.

When he woke up and there were twenty faces crowded around him, laughing and staring. The ground was cold and his backpack as propping one shoulder off the floor.

"All right class, back to your seats." Mrs. Johnson shooed the class away and began to fan Sam with a text book. She helped him sit up and looked him over with her mismatched eyes. "Welcome to Smithville," she said and the class let loose with another jolt of laughter. "I'm your biology teacher, Mrs. Johnson."

Sam shook his head and peeled his weakened body off the floor. He tried not to look at any of the students or the pig heads as he made his way to the back of the room to find a seat at an empty table. He thought he might throw up, but fought with every once of strength he had not to. This was already bad and he didn't need any more embarrassment for the day.

The rest of the morning was the same. Each period, a new class, more stares, and more embarrassment as he shuffled to find his seat. He carried his coat and backpack, not wanting to deal with finding his locker on his first day. Fifth period was lunch and Sam was surprised to find Molly sitting at a table with two other students chatting away. He bought a piece of pizza, an apple and some milk and carried his tray into the cafeteria. Molly was sitting on the far end, waving him over to sit with her.

Sam had never thought he would be happy see his twin sister, but after the morning he had, he was. He was making his way toward her table when all of the sudden he found the path blocked by what looked like a mountain in a wool sweater and canvas coat. His eyes rose up to a face – a crooked, mean face peering out from under a mane of thick black hair. This boy was enormous. Six feet at least. He looked like he was twenty years old, and even had a wispy mustache. He stood with his arms crossed across his barrel of a chest, his eyes burning into Sam, his breath reeking.

Here it was, Sam thought, the introduction the school bully.

"Where do you think you're going City Boy?" The voice was deep, as deep as Mr. Hutson's, and clinched. He had a toothpick sticking out the side of his mouth.

"Look, I don't want any trouble," Sam said. "I just want to eat my lunch, okay?"

"Did you hear that boys? City Boy just wants to eat his lunch." At that moment, Sam noticed two other mountains of men standing behind their leader. They all wore cowboy boots and tight jeans with big rodeo buckles. They had on wool shirts and sweaters under brown canvas jackets. In Chicago, they might have been a street gang. But here, Sam thought, they were just the guys to avoid.

"Well City Boy, we don't want to keep you from eatin' your lunch," said the big one in the center. "Do we?"

"No, not at all," the other two said in agreement.

"Here, let me help you." The leader took Sam's piece of pizza and rubbed it in his face while the whole lunch room stared in silence. Then he opened Sam's milk and poured it on his head and smushed the cake into the front of his light blue shirt. Every student in lunch room erupted with laughter as Sam tried not to cry. Molly rushed over and pushed the bully with little effect, screaming at him to leave her brother alone. But the bully just laughed and pushed Sam in the chest.

"I hope you enjoyed your lunch, City Boy," he said, and the three of them slinked away.

Molly tried wiping Sam off with napkins from his tray as he stood there motionless, listening to cackling laughter from the students in the room. She was wiping off the milk, when he suddenly dropped his tray and ran from the cafeteria. He needed to escape. He could feel tears welling up inside him and didn't want anyone else to see. He was more than embarrassed. He was angry, feeling betrayed – by his parents, by the move. Everything he had been holding in since that dinner a couple months before, when he found out they were moving, was coming rushing to the surface and all he wanted to do was run. Molly followed him, calling his name over the laughter.

Sam sprinted down the main hallway, turned the corner into the bathroom, ignoring a teacher telling him to slow down. Suddenly, he was falling backward, a thud echoing in his chest. He hit the ground hard and looked up to see the red backpack and curly blond hair disappear in the other direction. Twice in one day and par for the course, he thought. A tear began to tumble down his cheek as he pulled himself up and into the bathroom.

Molly was calling from outside, asking if he was okay. Sam stared at himself in the mirror. He was trying to wipe the cake out of his shirt and the pizza sauce from his cheek, but seemed only to be making it worse, when he noticed something in the mirror. In the stall behind him was something written on the wall, a message he did not understand – and on the ground next to it was a single long feather. Sam bent down to pick up the feather, milk still dripping in his ears. He looked it over. It was long and brown with white on the end. He looked it over closely until he heard Molly.

"That's it, I'm coming in there."

Sam stashed the feather in his book bag and turned to face his sister, who was grabbing paper towels and mumbling about arrogant jerks under her breath. She tended to him, but his mind was elsewhere. When things got rough, Sam tended to disappear into his own mind. He would shut down. When he was younger and his mom and dad would fight, he would block out the sound of them arguing and imagine himself on a great adventure. Sometimes when he would be cleaning his room or brushing his teeth, Molly would shake him and tell him he'd been standing there, staring off into space. But he had no awareness of time passing when he shut down – no concept of where he was. He might hear voices, but they sounded muffled. It was like his brain was a secret hiding place that only he could find. He didn't want to think about the bully, about the embarrassment of the morning, about how much he hated it here – and his mind protected him from thinking about those things. Instead, he couldn't stop thinking about the feather, about the words written on the wall.

"Sam! Sam! You're doing it again."

He was suddenly back in the bathroom, with his sister, who had wiped away most of the food and was telling him that they needed to go to Mr. Hutson to report what happened.

"We have to tell him. We have to call mom," she pleaded.

"No," Sam said. "No we're not talking about it. We're not calling anyone."

Just then the bell rang and Sam stepped out of the bathroom, leaving Molly where she stood. He went to class and while he didn't have another incident during the remaining three periods, he was not entirely present either. His mind kept drifting back to the feather, the words, the red backpack and curly blond hair.

In the car, after school, Sam stared quietly out the window at the passing rows of what once was corn while Molly explained in excited tones the events of the day. She told their mom all about the bully and Sam's milk shower and how the kids laughed and she had tried to stand up for him. She also told her all about class and the new kids she had met and how Mr. Hutson expects such great things from a student with her academic record.

"Are you alright Sam?" Mom was worried. He hadn't been himself since they moved; he hadn't been talking the way he had when they lived in Chicago. He hardly noticed her speaking to him; he just kept staring out the window thinking about the message written on the mirror in the bathroom:

Not all treasure is gold.

What did that mean? Was there some sort of treasure hidden in the school? And what did the feather have to do with it? Sam turned it over and over in his mind. He almost forgot about the terrifying and humiliating incident in the lunch room, about fainting in biology class, about how much he hated this place, the house, his room.

It was a strange thing to be there. That's what he kept coming to. Every junior high bathroom he'd ever been in had writing on the wall. Mr. Marx is a butthead. He who smelt it, dealt it. Here I was, I had a squat, but yours smells bad and mine does not. That kind of thing. Who would write something so mysterious? So cryptic? There had to be a reason why. It had to mean something. Then again, maybe it was nothing and he was clinging to the only thing that day that didn't make him wish he had never been born. And what about the boy with the blond curly hair? He had run Sam over, twice. The first time was after the first bell had rung, so the kid was probably running late. But the bathroom? There was no reason to run unless he was running away from something. Had he written the message on the wall? If so, why? Who did he want to read it? Could he have written it specifically for Sam? Again, why? And the feather?

Sam knew he was probably making connections that weren't real. He knew there was probably nothing to any of it, but part of him needed it to be a mystery. He needed it to be something other than what it was. He needed something in his life other than thinking about his old life and everything he had left behind.

"Sam!" Mom was nearly shouting. She had pulled the car over and was leaning into the back seat, shaking his arm. He was suddenly snapped back into the moment. "Are you alright? Molly told me everything. Are you okay?"

"Yeah, yeah, I'm fine." He actually had not given the incident in the lunch room much thought, except when the students in his afternoon classes giggled and pointed at the cake-stain on his shirt and his messy, milk-soaked hair. He had been pondering the message.

"Do you know that boy's name? I'm going to call his mother."

"No don't." He knew – just like every kid knows – that a mom getting involved would only make things worse. Panic shot through him like a warm electric wind. "It's nothing mom, just a little hazing on the new kid. Besides, it won't help."

She made him promise that if anything like that ever happened again he would tell her and they would meet with Mr. Hutson together. He really had no intention of telling her anything about what had happened in the lunchroom and hoped Molly would keep her mouth shut if anything happened again.

That night in bed, Sam laid awake looking at the feather. It was huge, as long as a ruler, and the color of dirt – with about two inches of white on the very tip. He had never seen a feather like it before. Back in Chicago he really only saw pigeons, so his experience with feathers was limited to short gray ones, sometimes with a little green on them. He wondered what kind of creature would have feathers like this. He tried an image search on his computer and even thumbed the pages of the encyclopedia, but what was he supposed to look up? Feathers? He looked at eagles and hawks and falcons and owls, but nothing seemed to match. There were birds with the same colors, but they didn't seem big enough for a feather like this one. The only thing might have been a match was an ostrich. But flightless birds native to Africa seemed a little far-fetched, even for a town as odd and foreign as Smithville.

He twirled the feather in his fingers while repeating the message over and over.

Not all treasure is gold.
Not all treasure is gold.
Not all treasure is gold.

He fell asleep thinking – having gotten no further than he was earlier in the day. What he did not think about was how much he hated his room. And for the first time since Chicago, he slept the whole night, dreaming about the message in the mirror and the feather in his backpack.

Chapter Three

Standing outside the entrance to Smithville Junior High, Sam once again felt like a deer transfixed by the headlights of an oncoming truck. But the deer doesn't know what the truck was, and Sam had a pretty good idea of what was waiting for him inside that school: embarrassment, humiliation and more feeling awkward and missing home. He thought about the bully. He was scared and worried that Molly's attempt to rescue him had only made him look like an even bigger loser than what he would have had she not stepped in. Best to try and find his locker, he thought. In the confusion and events of the day before he had never even looked. Finding his locker might give him something to do, a place to go, maybe even a place to hide. Just then a rush of students pulled him into the front entrance like a river current pulling a log downstream.

His locker was down near the end of the East hallway, next to Molly's. And she was there waiting for him when he arrived.

"Don't look at it, it will be okay," she said, trying to reassure him.

But he did look and was horrified. It was covered with magic marker and pieces of used gum. Go Home City Boy. Part of him wanted to laugh. Was that the best they had? But mostly he just felt his shoulders sag and his heart sink. How was it that an ignorant bully could find his locker before he had? And what had he done to deserve this? Apart from being forced to move and passing out in his first class and being treated like a garbage can in front of a few hundred strangers that he was supposed to, somehow, turn into friends? There were other, smaller notes, written on the locker door.

Chicago is for losers.

No gang-bangers in Smithville.

Gang banger? He had never been in a gang. He never even knew anyone in a gang. What was this all about? Again, he wondered how they knew which locker was his. Word travels fast in a town as small as Smithville, he thought, and he would just have to get used to being an outsider – to having everyone know everything they thought they knew about him.

A giant wad of pink gum made it impossible for Sam to turn the combination lock and he knew he would have to carry his books and coat the entire day. Molly offered to let him stash his things in her locker, but somehow he just couldn't deal with that. She said goodbye and squeezed his arm as if to apologize before heading off down the hall for her first class. Sam watched as she was joined by two girls who seemed excited to see his sister, like they had been friends for years.

There was no gum on Molly's locker, no hateful messages. Quite the opposite actually — a piece of paper decorated with glitter pen flowers and bright colors read "Welcome to SJH Molly! We're excited you're here." It was signed by at least ten girls, half of them, Sam noticed, used little hearts to dot the i's in their names.

He took a long deep breath and tried to psych himself up, then headed off to pig head-ology, his first class of the day. The scene was not as bad as it had been the day before, and he took small pleasure in making it to the back of the class, to his seat, without passing out.

Mrs. Johnson has assigned him a pig head the day before – a pink lump of skin stretched unevenly over bones. It's snout was crooked and one of its eyes was missing. Sam thought maybe all the good pig heads had been taken before he got there. It was a lab day, so that meant students removed their pig heads from the deep freezer in the corner of the room and spent the class working on them, dissecting them to little pieces and drawing what they found on lab sheets. Everyone else in the class had a partner, except for Sam, who was assigned one by Mrs. Johnson before they began.

"I hope you washed your hair," Jacob said, taking a seat next to Sam, who was delicately touching the pig head in front of him.

Sam said nothing and waited for the punch line.

"No, I mean it, because spoiled milk and pig brains are a bad combination. I heard that this kid from Rileyville was dissecting a pig head once and his mom had put milk in his lunch bag that he forgot was in his backpack. And bam. Pow. Plop. He puked his guts out all over the floor."

"I'm fine, thanks," said Sam, hoping his partner would change the topic or just shut up.

"That's why I won't do this stuff. I'm a conscientious objector when it comes to this stuff. I tell Mrs. Johnson I'm a vegetarian, which is only half-true since I mostly eat chips. But still, true story, I swear. Seriously," he said, looking down at the pig head. "Whoa, what is that, the brain? It's coming out of its eye, man. That's nasty!"

Sam shifted on the squeaky lab stool. He thought Jacob was hazing him, just trying to get him to react or throw up or pass out so that he could once again be the thing everyone laughed at.

"Look. Please stop," he said. "I'm trying to get this done."

"I wonder what it would look like if you cut the nose off. There'd probably be all kinds of boogers and stuff in there. And blood! And probably brain!"

Sam stood up and pushed his lab stool out from underneath him sending it crashing to the floor. The whole class stopped what they were doing and stared at him.

"I get it. I'm the new kid! I passed out yesterday! I get that no one wants me here and every one wishes I would just go back to Chicago!" He was yelling now. "Well guess what?! I wish I could go back to Chicago! I hate it here! This stupid school! This stupid town!"

"That's enough!" Mrs. Johnson called from the front of the room. She was making her way toward Sam's table, but he kept going.

"I know you just want to pick on me because I am new. I know you want to see me puke and pass out so that you can make fun of me and put more stuff in my hair and on my locker! But, you know what? I don't care!"

He pulled the tray containing the pig head off the table and flung it toward the center of the room, sending it sliding across the floor and hitting the far wall with a frozen thud. Sam then grabbed his backpack and coat and stormed from the room. He could hear Mrs. Johnson calling him back over the cackling laughter of the rest of the class as he rounded the comer and down the hall where his locker was.

"Stupid school. Stupid class," he muttered under his breath as he stormed down the empty hallway. "Stupid town. Stupid damn kids."

He didn't notice Mr. Hutson in the hall until he heard the booming voice.

"Son, that kind of language might be acceptable in the big city, but around here it earns you a trip to my office."

Mr. Hutson sent Sam down to his office and told him to wait there until he could see him. Sam's muttered tirade was only slightly interrupted as he continued to mumble to himself all the way to the office and more while he sat in the green chairs outside Mr. Hutson's inner sanctuary.

"Three detentions," Sam told Molly as they were walking toward the lunch room. "One lousy word and he gave me three detentions."

"Sam," Molly was delicate in how she spoke. She didn't want to upset her brother any more than he already was, but at the same time it really was his fault. "I, I don't want to sound too high and mighty, but you did do a little more than just say one bad word. I mean, tossing a pig's head? Running out of class and down the hall while Mrs. Johnson was talking to you? You probably got off light."

"I just hate it here. It stinks. The kids are all mean, it's boring and Mr. Hutson has it out for me."

"Really, I don't think its that bad," she was trying to lighten her brother's heavy heart. "The school is only two years old and a lot nicer than our old school. The teachers seem nice and I'm sure we'll have plenty of opportunities we never had in Chicago."

"Opportunities? Like what, boring ourselves to death?"

"Sam just because you had a bad couple of days doesn't mean that you won't end up liking it."

They arrived at the lunchroom door and Sam turned toward the line forming near where the food is handed out. Molly grabbed her brother's arm just as he was about to walk away.

"Are you going to be okay?"

"I'll be fine."

"Are you sure, because you can put your stuff in my locker if you want."

"Thanks, but I'll be fine."

Molly, who had gotten up early and packed her own lunch so she could avoid milk products – which she was allergic to – went into the cafeteria and sat down with some girls Sam recognized from English class. He swallowed hard and did his best to not look nervous as he entered the cafeteria line. He considered carefully the food he chose. Chicken noodle soup? No way, he was not going to be wearing a soup helmet for the rest of the afternoon. Toasted cheese would leave to big of a stain. He made his way down the line analyzing what the bullies could do with each of the foods. When he made it to the register and the lunch lady, Ms. Tallirude, added up his selection and asked, "Are you sure that's all you want for lunch?" Sam looked at his tray – a bowl of dry granola and a piece of toast. He was pretty sure there could not be much damage done with these items, so he paid Ms. Tallirude and took a deep breath before stepping into the cafeteria.

No one turned to look, no one turned to sneer. No one was laughing. Sam spotted Molly across the room and made his way toward her. He was nearly there and the coast was clear. He made one final check over his shoulder before he sat down at the table with his sister.

"Hey look everyone! City Boy is really a girl!"

The voice was familiar and an ominous sense of dread washed over Sam like a heavy rain. It was him, the bully, the one from yesterday. And he was getting closer. "City Boy likes to be one of the girls!"

"Look at me, I'm from Chicago! Aren't I pretty?" he said in a high-pitched voice and Sam could tell from the sound of it that he was standing right over his shoulder. And that's when he felt a pull on the collar of his shirt. It was a hand, a huge hand, the same hand that the day before had spread pizza across his face and cake on his chest. Sam soon found himself standing and spinning around to face the Bully, who was wearing an army jacket and his big freckled face was right in front of Sam's. His breath smelled like cat food and toilet water, his teeth looked like jagged cliffs atop the mountain of his body. He was pulling Sam up by the collar, lifting him right off the ground.

"City Boy here didn't learn his lesson yesterday," the Bully said and he began making that hocking guttural sound, the one that told Sam he was about to have a monumental loogie spit in his face. Sam didn't have time to think. He didn't even know how to react. With his mind dizzy with fear and anxiety, his body took over. It was fight or flight, kill or be killed – and mother nature has a way of making somebody choose kill. Without knowing it, Sam's knee jerked upward just as the Bully was rearing back to fire his projectile into the 12-year-old's face.

One motion, quick and fierce. One small movement and – CONTACT! Sam's eyes shot to the size of tea saucers when he felt the blow, his knee, his poor little knee that survived cuts and scrapes during years of blacktop baseball with his friends had connected with the giant's groin in a meaningful way. Sam almost felt the recoil, like the kick from a shotgun and immediately the Bully, this Goliath crunched in half, felled by David's slingshot. Or in this case Sam's knee to the family jewels. He left go of Sam's shirt and Sam fell awkwardly backwards, landing and sliding on his butt across the lunchroom floor. He popped up immediately to watch the slow-motion ballet of the Bully doubling over and falling stiffly to the ground. It seemed like it took an hour for the towering oaf to fall and when he hit the ground a shockwave sent shivers through the room, which was deathly silent.

Sam watched the giant fall then looked to his two compadres, who were coming out of the shock of seeing their leader fall and turning their attention to Sam, their eyes burning with ferocity.

"Get … him," the Bully gasped.

Sam looked at Molly who told him to run, run away, run fast, run hard and don't stop! Like a leopard, Sam bolted over Molly's table and set loose down the hall. The bumbling giants bumped into each other, but eventually began their pursuit. They began to gain on Sam in the main hallway. Sam looked over his shoulder and all of the sudden a frozen pig head zoomed across the freshly-waxed floor, followed closely by another one. Sam looked over his shoulder to see the frozen heads knock his pursuers to the ground. They fell, both of them, into a crumbled mess and Sam saw two students running after him, telling him to hurry up.

One of them was Jacob, the other a small boy with brown hair. Both wore enormous smiles and seemed to be joining Sam, rather than chasing him.

"Did you see that Zachary? Did you see? They fell like a pile of bricks!" Jacob was yelling to the boy next to him. "Sam! Did you see that? Seven-ten split, we picked up the spare! Got 'em! Butt-head bowling! Too cool!"

The three boys bolted out the door at the end of the hall and across the soccer field to the woods that lined the school property – safe it would seem, for a little while at least.

Chapter Four

Zachary took the lead with Jacob right behind him and Sam trying to keep up. They were running up a trail, leading them deeper into the woods. Sam's lungs were starting to bum from the heavy breathing and the cold January air. His legs were pumping and it felt odd to have beads of sweat running down his face in the middle of winter, but it felt good to run; he felt like himself again. Zachary and Jacob disappeared around a comer and Sam followed them, almost knocking them over when he turned the bend to find them stopped at the base of a tree.

Zachary started climbing a ladder – pieces of wood pounded into the side of the tree – and Jacob followed. Sam, who still had no idea what had happened, followed. They had not said a word to each other in the last six and a half minutes they had been running. At the top of the ladder was a fort made out of scrap pieces of two-by-four and plywood most likely stolen from a construction site somewhere. The fort was made up of a single room with large openings on each side covered with makeshift shades – pieces of plywood attached by hinges. A small walkway went around the outside and one of the 'windows' overlooked a clearing. Sam shimmied his way into the fort just as Jacob and Zachary were opening the windows. Sam crouched in a comer and pulled his coat on.

"I think we're safe now Zachary," Jacob was panting and looking out cautiously. Zachary nodded, not saying anything, but implying an affirmative response to Jacob's comment.

"Safe from what?" Sam asked. "Where did you guys come from?"

Jacob pulled up an apple crate from the comer and had a seat, Zachary moved from window to window, double-checking that they had not been followed.

"Safe from the Williams gang, of course."

"What's the Williams gang?"

"The Williams gang, my friend, is the group of gargoyles you just narrowly escaped, thanks to us. Butch Williams is their leader, the one you nailed right in the nuts! That was awesome!"

Jacob seemed delighted by Sam's instinctive self-defense. "Bart and Bud are Butch's cousins. They're the ones who accidentally slipped on the pig noggins we bowled at 'em."

Sam could not help but smile. He tried to hold it back, but enjoyed the image of the pig heads sliding across the floor like bowling balls, knocking the legs out from beneath Bart and Bud Williams. They fell on top of each other and on top of the craniums. Two perfect shots and Sam saved his hide.

"Yeah, thanks for that."

"No problem, buddy, it was our pleasure. We've wanted to get back at those guys since last summer when we were swimming in the quarry and they stole our clothes. We had to walk all the way back to town in our underwear."

Sam wondered how Jacob and Zachary could have possibly known he was running down the hall. Had they been in the cafeteria, there was no way they could have gotten to Mrs. Johnson's room and back with the pig heads by the time he made it half-way down the hall. He thought about asking, but thought maybe he should apologize for his outburst in class earlier that morning first.

"Look Jacob, I'm sorry about this morning."

"No problem man. I didn't realize you would get so freaked out. I was just trying to make you feel welcome."

Just then Zachary stopped his century march around the outside of the fort and snapped his fingers inside the window. Jacob stopped talked and spun around, dipping below the level of the window, only to peer over in the direction of the clearing.

"Zachary, that's him."

Sam thought for sure Butch had found them. His life flashed before his eyes. Birth, Chicago, baseball, fighting with Molly, moving to Smithville. His knee, the pig heads. It was all about to end because a brick wall of pubescent angst was about to come crashing down on him. It had been a good life ... for the most part.

He nudged his way toward the window and stuck his nose just over the ledge. When he focused on the brightly lit, snow-covered opening, he was surprised to see a newly familiar sight as a red backpack and blonde curly hair dashed across the far-end of the clearing and into the trees beyond.

"Hey, who is that kid?"

"Sssshhhhhh. We're not out of the woods here Sam, let's try and keep our voices down."

Jacob and Zachary passed a knowing glance between them and as Zachary walked back around the outside of the fort to the door. Jacob took his new friend by the shoulder and sat him down, like a grandfather about to explain the secret mysteries of the universe to a young impressionable child.

They sat, the three of them in the center of the fort, Jacob atop his apple basket, the teacher about to give a lesson.

"That kid? We'll get to that kid later. First, I think you better learn the lay of the land at Smithville Junior High. A little bit of knowledge about who is who is going to go a long way toward preventing future incidents like we had here this morning."

Sam wanted to know about the boy with the red backpack and he still was not sure that he should trust Jacob. But he had just saved his life, so maybe he was willing to give him a chance. It might be nice to have a friend in this town, he thought, someone to watch my back, someone to talk to – though he got the distinct feeling that Zachary didn't do much talking at all.

The next day, Sam met Jacob and Zachary in the loft above the lunchroom. It was dusty and a little dank and Mr. Hutson and other teachers used it as an observation post during dances. They stood up there, sipping coffee looking for trouble like some kind of prison guards. Jacob and Zach used it for their own personal lunchroom, a place to get away from the stresses of every day seventh grade life at Smithville JH.

From their perch, Jacob laid out the school in terms of who was who, who to talk to and who to avoid. In the far left corner were the jocks, football players mostly, but some wrestlers too. They pretty much kept to themselves, except on game day when they picked an unsuspecting nerd and stuffed something – usually involving Jell-O – down their pants. They thought it brought them luck. The jocks weren't much of a problem, Jacob explained, because they were usually too busy talking about sports and putting each other down to reach out into the world. They weren't known for their academic prowess, nor for their social graces.

Basically, you were a jock by birth or you were never a jock at all. Not all football players were jocks and not all jocks were on the team, Jacob explained. Being a jock meant having a sense that each day, every time the sun rose, it would not set until a football game was played. There were other athletes at the school, sure, but only a select few were jocks. Basketball players could not be jocks unless they were born jockey and played football as well. Then there were the mascots. No, not the ones who put on the badger costume and lead people in cheers, but the people who wished deep within them that they were jocks. Jocks sometimes opened up to these people, but not as equals – more like as a fan club. There were girl mascots and boy mascots. The girls usually had it easier, but sometimes a boy, like Roger Culbertson, could be a mascot.

Roger was a sports encyclopedia and Jacob said he came from a rough home. His mom was not around a lot and he never met his dad. His step-dad, Carl he thought his name was, was a jock; he played quarterback at Smithville High School twenty years ago. But now he just sort of sat around all day, complaining when Roger's mom didn't have dinner ready and drinking beer while watching reruns of games on television. Roger needed someone to look up to and he loved sports, so he was sort of an unofficial jock.

Jacob dismissed this group as a waste of time. They could be avoided, but breaking into their close knit group would be too much trouble for what it was worth. He moved on the next group of tables, in the far right corner of the lunchroom, where a group of lonely looking boys were huddled, leaning on the table, their knees in their chairs, and their elbows beneath their chests. Sam could see dice being thrown and cards being traded. These had to be the fantasy freaks, he thought. Every school had them – a tight group of boys, usually smarter than the average, who spoke in a language foreign to anyone outside their group. These guys lived for card games like Dungeons and Dragons and books that involved elves and fairies and far-away planets. They were harmless and nice, but they often drew the attention of people like the jocks who singled them out for being physically weaker. Sam had already learned that nerds should not be messed with too badly since they usually ended up changing the world like Bill Gates, or running the show like baseball general manners.

The beautiful people sat in the center of the room and the farmers on the near left. The near right was reserved for the artists. Jacob was explaining how the artists usually wore black and did strange things like suddenly break into French in mid-conversation – when Sam saw her. She was tall and blonde, with hair down past her shoulders and a face so perfect it appeared carved right from Sam's imagination. She was talking to another girl, one Sam recognized because she was sitting with Molly the day before. He watched her, nearly forgetting to breathe. It was as if all at once he was transported to a room without air, bright and white. His stomach began turning in knots while he watched her select a seat at the table next to his sister's. (Molly sat near the center of the room, within striking distance of the artists and the nerds, but closer to the beautiful people.)

By comparison, Sam thought, "the beautiful people" were ugly as he watched the girl flip her hair back and unpack her lunch bag. She had a sandwich. He loved sandwiches. And a juice box – his favorite! She seemed to move in slow motion, like a television commercial for shampoo, and there was a white halo around her. Sam wondered for a second if he could tear his eyes away – not that he wanted to, but he doubted whether he could. He was drawn, no pulled, toward her.

"Sam! Earth to Sam!" Jacob sort of sang as he tried to snap his new friend out of it. "Zachary, I think he's in a coma or something."

Sam's eyes were fixed open and it looked sort of like he was starting to drool. Jacob turned to Zachary and shrugged. Zachary saw his moment and opened the bottle of water he had in his backpack – dumping it on Sam's head. Sam was pulled back to real-life with a cold jolt.

"Sam! Wake up man!" Jacob was saying as he stood over Sam, trying not to get wet. The halo disappeared, air re-entered Sam's lungs and life returned to normal speed. "What's up man? Where'd you go?"

Sam wiped the water from his wet hair and the drool from the corner of his mouth. "Who is that?" he looked at the girl and pointed without being obvious.

"Who? That?" Jacob gave him a look like 'you've got to be kidding me' and turned to Zachary as if to say 'this guy can not be serious.' "That is only the object of a young man's dreams. That is only a girl so perfect she can only be described as a goddess, man. That is Amy Connor."

"She's beautiful."

"No duh? I guess they're right – you city boys are a whole lot smarter than us poor country folk," Jacob faked a hick accent. "Look man, many men have tried. Better men than you and I. They've tried, but all have failed. Besides, she's got a boyfriend who goes to boarding school in Massachusetts or Manhattan or something like that. She was a model, man. A model! Just forget about her. She is waaaaayyyyy out of your league. She's like in a different sport man, on another planet. She would not give a guy like you the time of day."

Sam was only half-listening to Jacob. A goddess, yup. A model, got it. Something, something, something. His head felt like his brain had just turned to scarf wool and his stomach felt like a fleet of sailboats were sloshing back and forth.

Chapter Five

Over the next few weeks, Sam settled into a routine at school. He tried to keep his head down and avoid the hallways as much as possible, for fear of an unfortunate run-in with the Williams gang. He went to his locker after every other period, rotating every other day. On Monday, Wednesday and Friday, it was after first, third, fifth and seventh period. On Tuesday and Thursday it was after second, fourth, sixth and eighth. He ate his lunches with Jacob and Zachary in the booth above the cafeteria and kept his eye on the lunchroom while they talked. Every once in a while, the Williams boys would ask Molly where her brother was, but other than that, they left him alone. There was another new kid in town and they seemed to be focused on him. He also liked to watch for Amy, who sat in the same seat every day, with the same lunch. Though he felt less like he might pass out every time he saw her, his head still swirled a little just at her sight.

One time he saw her in the library. She was a few aisles away, looking in the encyclopedias while he was looking up books on American History for a class project. He almost talked to her, but could not find the nerve.

Jacob and Zachary had helped him to acclimate to Smithville, showing him around town – the sporting goods store, the arcade, even an abandoned mill down by the river. He had put the feather into a tennis ball tube and hid in his closet after his first week of school and had nearly forgotten about it until one afternoon, right after the snow had melted and the weather warmed up enough that they could explore the woods without wearing heavy parkas. Jacob and Zachary were explorers by nature – at least Jacob was, and Zachary seemed content to follow.

Sam was trying to find things he had in common, which at first was limited to the fact that he was looking for friends and they were willing to talk to him. But the more he got to know them, the more Sam realized they were alike.

But he still missed Chicago. He missed eating dinner over at his friends' houses or having them spend the night. He got together with Jacob and Zachary – who he now called Jake and Zach – primarily after school for an hour or two, and then they went home. He spent weekends at home with his parents and Molly, doing homework or watching basketball on the finally installed satellite TV. Sometimes they went out to dinner or ordered pizza; but mostly, he just spent time in his room reading and daydreaming about this and that and Amy Connor.

Sam was half-reading the instructions on his math homework when he heard a knock on his bedroom door.

"Sam? Sammy honey can I come in?" His mom sounded delicate behind the door.

"Sure," he said and sat up. His mom was carrying a laundry basket full of clean clothes under her arm and a bag of cookies in her free hand. She put the laundry on his desk and sat down next to him on his bed.

"These came for you today, I ordered them special from Capozzi's deli back home." They still thought of Chicago as home. She handed him the cookies, peanut butter chocolate chip. His favorite. She put hand on his back and began to rub as he dug into the cookies. "Are you alright?"

Sam didn't know how to answer, other than to say 'sure' without taking his eyes out of the cookie bag.

"I mean, are you doing okay? It just seems like you're lonely. I want to make sure you're going to be okay. I know moving was really hard for you."

Sam was getting nervous. He never really knew what to say when his mom asked him things like this. He missed Chicago. He missed it a lot. Back there he felt like someone. Here, he hid during lunch and carried too many books to each class. He was secretly in love with a girl he had never talked to and his only friends were two guys who would rather shove straws down frogs' throats and blow them up than play baseball in the park. In fact he didn't even know where a baseball field was.

"I want you to know that your father and I are here for you if you need to talk," she said. "I'm fine mom, I really am." He wanted this conversation to end.

"It's just that Molly seems to be settling in so well. I mean right now she's over at a friend's house to spend the night. She's getting involved with things at school and seems happy. You just seem lonely. You spend all weekend in your room and other than an hour or so with some friends I've never met, you never go out."

Sam knew she was not trying to compare him to his twin sister. She would never do that, but he could not help but feel a little defensive.

"I said I'm fine," though he could feel his face getting red and his eyes welling up with tears.

"I've got an idea," she said. "Why don't you call your friends and ask them if they can spend the night here tonight. We'll rent you guys some stupid movies and get pizza and ice cream and you can stay up all night talking about whatever you want. I won't tell you to go to bed or anything."

Ordinarily Sam didn't like it when his mom made suggestions about his social life, but given the circumstances, a little bit of company sounded kind of nice.

"Okay," he resigned. "That sounds good. I'll call them."

His mom kissed him on the cheek just to embarrass him a little. She was relieved that he agreed to her idea and seemed to bounce out of the room. Jake had to ask his mom, but Zach knew he would be allowed since his parents were out of town at a State Fair Planning Board meeting and he was home with his sister. She was senior at Smithville High and would do anything to get rid of her little brother for the night. They all decided to meet at the video store downtown and Sam's mom called ahead to order the pizzas.

"I really appreciate your inviting us over Mrs. Drake," Jacob said as they piled into the backseat of the car. "I've been telling Sammy here that we need to spend some more social time together – you know to get away from school and the stress."

Jake had a way of talking to adults. He sort of sounded like one. Zach, who had a giant gobstopper that he bought at a vending machine in the pizza parlor stuffing the right side of his mouth, managed a grunted 'yeah thanks' as an echo to Jake's eloquence.

"No problem boys. I've looked forward to meeting the two of you for a while now."

"Oh the pleasure is all mine. And let me be the first of Sammy's friends to welcome your family to Smithville. I understand that moving can be a bit traumatic and difficult for families, especially when it is such a drastic change from your last environment, but we hope you find our little burg a welcoming and warm place to live."

Great, thought Sam, now he's the freaking welcome wagon. He looked at Zach and they both rolled their eyes.

"What movies did you get guys?"

"Just some horror flicks," answered Sam.

"Just some flicks?" Jacob asked. "Just some horror flicks? Why my friend, these are modern classics. Werewolves and zombies, these are the movies of legends."

Jake continued to lay it on pretty thick the rest of the way home. All the way up to Sam's room, he kept telling Mrs. Drake how lovely her decor was and how nice she had made things and how well it seems the family has settled in. She was carrying the pizza and pop, and Jake made sure there was not a single gap in conversation – or his monolog – while she was in his presence. When she left them to their food and films in Sam's room, Sam had to ask.

"What the heck was that all about?"

"What do you mean?"

"Why gee Mrs. Drake, what a lovely home you have and I love that shirt your wearing. Is that a ketchup stain? It suits you!" Sam was mocking Jake and Zach folded his hands next to his cheek, batting his eyelashes and making a kiss-kiss face.

"Shut up!"

"Butt-kisser!"

"You simply don't appreciate the importance of getting off on the right foot, making a good impression there Mr. Faints-at-the-sight-of-a-pig-head."

Point taken. They each took a place on the floor and a piece of pizza. Jake picked the first movie and put it into the DVD player/television combo sitting on a low table against the wall opposite Sam's bed.

The movie was called Attack of the Bear People and was one that Sam had never seen before. He liked scary movies, even though he could almost never sleep after watching them. It was in black and white and was set in a small town in the middle of nowhere on a dark and stormy night. As if to amplify the drama, an early-spring thunderstorm was starting to blow outside. The rain was pelting Sam's bedroom windows and lighting occasionally cast ominous shadows on the slanted ceiling.

In the movie, a high school boy and girl were on a date at a diner downtown, the kind you think of when you think about the 1950s. They shared a coke and French fries and everything seemed to be going pretty well until they decided to go for a drive up to lover's lane.

"This can't be good," said Jake. "It never is when you decide to drive into the woods on a night like that."

Sam gulped his coke and watched without blinking.

"What are they thinking?" Jake said as they turned off the main road onto the muddy dirt lover's lane. "I mean didn't they read the newspaper about the hiker that went missing? All they found was his boot and his foot was still in it? How could they possibly think this is a good idea?"

There is no logic when it comes to the heart, thought Sam – and for a moment Amy flashed into his mind.

The lovers reached an overlook atop a wooded hill and the boy – Cliff – parked the car. He put his arm around his girl –

Sally – and she leaned her head into his. They were just about to kiss when all of the sudden the car shook. There was an eerie silence for a second as the two lovers looked out the passenger side window for what had caused the disturbance. They seemed to relax for just a second when bam! A bloody paw attached to a human arm slapped across the windshield.

Sam and Jake jumped, but Zach kept his eyes glued to the TV, biting absently at his pizza. There was a loud roar and the driver's door flew open. Bart was dragged from the car and Sally screamed as the roaring mixed with the terrified screams of her date. She opened the passenger door and ran into the woods screaming.

She reached a clearing in the woods and stopped to catch her breath. The moon was cutting through the trees. She thought for a second she was safe – until she heard a branch snap. And out of the woods came a dozen creatures that were half-bear/half-human. They had bear heads and chests, but human arms and legs that ended in giant clawed paws. They walked upright and approached her from all directions. She tried running one way, but was blocked. She tried another, but was blocked there. As she tried to escape, the bear people drew closer and closer until they finally closed the circle and pounced on her.

Sam wanted to sit up and slap the television off, but he could not move; he was glued to the floor. He tried to look away, but didn't want to make it too obvious so Jake and Zach would make fun of him. Instead he squinted his eyes so they were nearly shut, opening them every couple of seconds. He could tell the guys he was blinking, that's all, he wasn't scared at all.

He was lying to himself without even being asked. He was scared. Terrified.

As the town's people organized a lynch mob to comb the forest in search of whatever had committed such a brutal act on the reverend's daughter, Sam could feel his heart pump loudly in his chest. He needed to pee, but the idea of leaving his room and venturing into the hallway alone was more than he could handle. He imagined stepping quickly into the hall toward the bathroom, making it in there and closing the door quickly behind him. He'd lock the door and feel safe for a moment until, just as he began to relax, the shower curtain would burst open and huge paw at the end of a man's arm would come flying toward his face. That would be the last thing he ever saw. And the kids at school would remember him as the boy who died because he had to pee.

Sam decided to hold it and flexed every muscle in his body to keep from wetting his jeans. He wondered if Jake and Zach could tell he was trying to dam the flood waters, alternating between squinting at the screen and squirming on the floor.

The movie ended with one lonely hero slaying the leader of the bear people, breaking the spell that had cursed a dozen lonesome travels to a carnivorous life as a part-bear. The hero was strong and handsome with a cleft in his chin that made Jake think of a butt. Captain Buttface he mumbled when the tattered hero – his hair still perfectly quaffed – returned to the town to reassure the villagers they were once and for all safe.

When the movie ended, Jake stood up and turned on the lamp next to the television then rewound the tape. He looked so perfectly at peace and Sam knew that he did not.

"What's the matter Sammy? You look like you seen a ghost."

"I'm fine," said Sam.

"Is Sammy scared Zach?" Zach nodded and began to giggle a little. He too was not frightened by the movie.

"I'm not scared," protested Sam. "That wasn't scary."

He noticed that the violent urge to pee had for the moment subsided.

"Those kinds of things aren't scary. I mean, bear-people? Come on." Sam was trying to convince himself just as much as he was trying to convince his friends. "Yeah, like that's realistic. That could never happen, so what's there to be scared about?"

Jake and Zach shot each other a knowing look. After a moment of silence in which Sam's thoughts again returned to his bladder, Jake nodded to Zach who nodded back to Jake and then toward Sam.

"What is it?" Sam asked.

"It's just that," Jake paused. "It's just that bear-people might not be possible, but that does not mean something like that could not happen."

"Part humans, part animals?" Sam nudged himself onto the bed without fully standing up. "You've got to be kidding me."

Jake broke eye contact with Sam and looked at the floor as if he were debating in his head whether or not to go on.

"Actually, it can happen and it does happen," his voice trailed off for a second.

Sam looked at Jake and then at Zach, he was beginning to think that his friends were putting him on.

"You guys are messing with me."

"Sam, do you remember the day we rescued you from the Williams boys?"

"Yeah."

"Do you remember when you asked us about the kid with the red backpack and we didn't tell you anything?"

Sam's thoughts flashed to the feather in his closet and without being specific about what, he instantly got scared.

"Yeah."

"Well, maybe its time we told you about Jack."

Great, thought Sam, now I'm never going to the bathroom.

Chapter Six

Jake stood in the center of Sam's room, the only light coming from the lamp behind him, making his face hard to see. Sam sat on the bed and Zach at the desk, lazily spinning on Sam's desk chair. When lighting struck outside, Jake's face was momentarily lit a pale blue. This was going to be scarier than the movie.

The story went something like this, according to Jake. Jack Jacobs, the boy with the red backpack and blonde curly hair, used to be a popular kid. He was a football player, the best quarterback in the Pee Wee league. He was the captain of his junior hockey team, a straight-A student, and the best looking boy at Smithville Elementary. He was in Jake's class and was a heck of guy. People looked up to him, even at that early age. All the girls had a crush on Jack and he was nice to everyone. Everyone, even the kids who sit at the nerd table for lunch. He never made fun of other kids. He never missed a day of class. He was perfect.

One day, near the end of the summer between fifth and sixth grade, Jack was in the woods hiking with his brother Craig. Craig was two years older and just like Jack. He was the king of Smithville Junior High, but never acted like it. Jack looked up to Craig a lot. He wanted to be just like him. They used to play football in the front yard of their parents' house out on route 38 near the state park, which is where they were hiking that day.

"Nobody really knows the details of what happened," Jake said. "But it was bad. Really bad."

Jake explained how Jack and Craig were climbing a trail to the ridge. The trail was bending and getting more and more narrow. Craig was in the lead and Jack was following him, falling slightly farther behind with every step his bigger, older brother took. Craig pushed forward and had rounded a bend in the trail. They say Jack never saw it coming. How could he? How could he expect that something like that would happen?

"What happened?" asked Sam, sounding a bit more sheepish than what he would have liked.

"Craig got taken."

"Taken?"

"Carried off. Taken away. He was snatched by something not quite human, but not quite animal either."

Sam's heart began to pound as he pictured the scene in his head. A bigger kid – who had finished eighth grade and was going on to high school – carried off. He suddenly felt small and crunched down toward the end of his bed, wanting to get away from the window.

"Wh-uh, what was it?"

"There really isn't a name for it," Jake said. "I heard Jack only saw a part of it as it carried Craig off into the woods. It had wings and talons like an eagle, but its face was like a person. It grabbed Craig by the shoulders and flew off with him."

Sam tried to swallow, but his throat was dry.

"Jack Jacobs has not been the same since," said Jake. "Now he just sort of keeps to himself. He doesn't play football or have any friends. He's not even always in class."

Sam thought about his three encounters with Jack. He'd been knocked over twice and had seen him across the field the day he kneed Butch in the marbles.

"Did they ever find him?"

"Who? Craig? Nope. There was no trace. He just sort of disappeared. Except for that backpack that Jack carries around. Some people think that's why Jack's always running off into the woods – to try and find him. But since he never talks to anyone anymore, no one really knows."

Sam thought more about the feather in the tennis ball can tucked in the comer of his closet. He thought of how Jack must have found it on the ground as he watched the giant bird man take his brother off to a certain and grim fate. He had never mentioned the feather or the message to anyone, but he suddenly felt overcome by the desire to tell both Jake and Zach.

"I found a feather," he blurted out, taking his friends by surprise. "I found it and it was Jack's and it must belong to the thing that took Craig off."

Jake appeared awestruck by this revelation. Even Zach, who usually maintained a cool, calm disposition seemed troubled at the news.

"You found what?"

"A feather. I was in the bathroom on my second day at school and Jack knocked me over and I found it on the floor."

"Well, where is it?" Jacob asked. He seemed cautious, but eager. He had no idea Sam had such an important artifact.

Sam got off the bed and walked to the closet. He pulled the tennis ball can from its place in the back left corner – behind the shiny black Sunday shoes his mom bought him, but that never really fit. He was careful moving it, like it was a bomb or a test tube full of a deadly virus. He held it with one hand on top and the other gently cradling the bottom and set it on the bed. Jake and Zach moved closer to get a good view of what Sam was about to show them.

Pulling the lid off, Sam reached into the can with two fingers – his index and thumb – and gently grasped the tip of the white feathers. For some reason he thought it would be heavier, being that it carried the weight of murder, but it was a feather after all. Jake and Zach put their noses close to get a closer look, but neither made a move to touch it. Zach had his hands in his jeans pockets and Jake held his behind his back, like an art lover observing a famous painting in some big city museum.

"Start from the beginning," Jake said. "Go slow and don't leave anything out."

Sam told them about his first run-in with Jack Jacobs, standing outside the school on his very first day. And how he had knocked him over for the second time in the bathroom. He told them about the message and carrying the feather in his backpack. He told them everything, every detail, even how Molly stood outside the door then came in to see if Sam was alright.

"Has she seen the feather?"

"I don't think so."

"Good. Let's keep it that way. Have either of you spoken about Jack? I mean, do you think she's seen him?"

"Probably not. She's got friends and school work. She doesn't really think about that kind of stuff."

Jake, Sam and Zach each took a closer look at the feather before Sam put it back in the tennis ball can and sealed the lid. He left it on the bed and the three of them began discussing their next move. The rest of the movies would just have to wait.

Chapter Seven

The boys had agreed to not tell anyone about the things they had seen and talked about. Not yet anyway. The situation was too delicate. They would pretend nothing was going on when they were at school – talking about things seventh grade boys talk about, getting ready for the Smithville spring fest and eating their lunch in the perch as usual.

Sam tried to concentrate on school, but often he found himself daydreaming, or something very close to it. He was awake, but somewhere else. When he walked down the halls, his mind was lost in a dream or an image, like a movie playing in his head. He was hiking up a trail, following a red backpack and shocks of curly blonde hair. He could barely keep up. He was gasping and he could feel sweat dripping hard down his forehead. He was hiking as fast as he could, almost running up the narrow trail, still he could not seem to keep up. Something was pulling him back, like a weight or a giant hanging on his shirt, making it harder and harder to keep up. He kept pumping his legs but fell farther and farther behind, the red backpack getting smaller and smaller in front of him, until its gone, vanishing around a bend in the upward slope of the trail.

"Earth to Sam. Are you alive Sam?"

Sam was snapped back to reality. He realized he was standing in front of his locker, Molly looking right at him as if he were some kind of alien.

"Are you okay? Sam?"

"What? Oh, yeah."

He hadn't noticed that Molly was not alone. Standing next to her was the face of an angel, the Helen that would make him bum Smithville Junior High like some kind of Troy. Amy Connor. He had not consciously thought about her since that night in his room with Jake and Zach, but he supposed she never really left his mind.

"I want you to meet a friend of mine," said Molly, still looking at her brother as if he were something other than himself. "This is Amy Connor. She's in our English class, but I don't think you two have met."

Sam went from racing in a spooky dream to feeling like he might faint. He held it together though and managed to smile a half-cocked smile.

"It's nice to meet you Sam," Amy said. Even her voice sounded like that of an angel, he thought. "Yeah, uh, uh, nice to meet you too." He fumbled.

Molly rolled her eyes, knowing that her brother was swooning on the inside.

"Well, anyway, Amy and I were thinking about going out to the State Park this weekend to do some hiking and I thought I would ask if you and your little friends would like to come."

The state park. Sam's thoughts were like a laser. They could not possibly go to the state park, not with a boy-eating, half-human, half-eagle out there on the loose.

"No!" He blurted. Molly looked shocked.

"What, we move to this town and all of the sudden you're too good to hang out with your sister?"

"No, wait, Molly. That's not what I meant. I just meant that it's been raining a lot lately and hiking is probably a bad idea. Mudslides and all."

"Mudslides?" Amy asked – Molly appeared to be thinking the same thing.

"Oh yes. Mudslides. They come out of nowhere and can be very dangerous you know."

"Well what do you suggest we do then?" Molly asked.

"We could, um, go to the arcade or something."

"Great," said Amy. "It's a date. We'll go to the arcade on Friday night."

"Yeah. Great."

"See you in English." "Yeah. See you in English."

Molly and Amy walked off to class and Sam could not believe what had just happened. A date? A date with Amy Connor?

This was awesome. Sure it also involved Molly, Jake and Zach, but she said date. He heard it. SHE called it a DATE.

"So City Boy's got a date, huh? Did you hear that boys?"

Butch's voice was like a lion's roar cutting right through Sam. He turned around and looked right into the buttons of the Williams gang's shirts.

"I guess City Boy is also a lover boy, isn't that right boys?"

The whole gang nodded. Sam could not make a sound. All of the air had left his lungs, and fast. "Friday night at the arcade. I guess we'll see you there City Boy. And don't think I've forgotten what happened in the lunchroom."

The Williams gang each took a turn bumping hard into Sam as they slinked off down the hall. He was dumbstruck and as the bell rung, he was overcome with three distinct feelings: fear, love and more fear.

Chapter Eight

"I still can't believe you're going through with this."

Jake, Sam and Zach were walking across the square in the middle of downtown Smithville toward the arcade.

"I mean you said Butch basically told you he was going to flatten you if you showed up tonight."

Sam was walking confidently, even if he was terrified on the inside. It would be worth it to get his butt kicked if it meant he got to spend time with Amy. Jake kept talking nervously as they crossed the central Smithville Square – where the Soldiers and Sailors monument stood and concerts were held in the summer. Molly and Amy were standing outside the arcade, having gotten a ride from Amy's dad. Sam's throat went dry the closer they got. His palms were a little sweaty and he worried the deodorant he put on might not be enough to cover the smell if he started to sweat.

The arcade was in a building that once held a movie theatre. The Rialto went out of business when the new 19-screen Megaplex went up out on the north side of town. The arcade quickly moved in, despite some protest from downtown residents who worried that such a business might bring the wrong element to town. The marquee was still lit with same dull orangish bulbs it had been lit with when the theater was still open – casting dark, ominous shadows on the sidewalk and on people's faces as they stood beneath it. Even in this dark light, Amy was beautiful, wearing a white sweater and khaki shorts. Sam hardly noticed his twin sister standing there.

"Oh hi Molly," he said trying not to stare at Amy, but it was hard.

"Aren't you going to introduce us?" She asked. She nodded her head sideways toward Jake and Zach, who both had dressed as nicely as possible for the occasion. It was not every day that they spent time with girls, even if it was a friend's sister and the object of his desire.

"You must be Molly," Jake started with his first impression act. "Sam has told me so much about you. I feel like we've known each other for years. He failed to mention how beautiful you are, however – a trait you must get from your mother, a charming woman I had the pleasure of meeting the other day."

He introduced himself as Jacob and his esteemed colleague Zachary. He nodded a brief hello to Amy and Zach smiled.

"Charmed, I'm sure," Molly said, dismissing Jake and staring a beat too long at Zach. "Should we go inside?"

The inside of the arcade was a blinding labyrinth of blinking neon and flashing strobe lights, with loud noises coming from every dark corner. Jake insisted on buying Molly some tokens and soon the three of them were off playing games, leaving Sam and Amy to themselves. They waited in line in awkward silence to get tokens.

"So Molly tells me you used to play baseball in Chicago."

Sam was startled. She, this goddess, knew something about him. She was asking him a question. Don't say something stupid, he thought. Don't say something stupid. DO NOT SAY ANYTHING STUPID.

"Uh, yeah." He said it sideways, afraid to look her in the eye.

"That's cool. There aren't many boys around here who play baseball. Every body is so wrapped up in football or farming. I always liked baseball. I used to go to games with my dad when we lived in Cleveland."

Cleveland? That means she's not native. Sam had never considered that there could be other people in Smithville who were not from Smithville. He felt the belt around his chest – the one that had made it feel hard to breath whenever he saw Amy – start to loosen up.

"So I guess that means you're an Indians' fan?" He looked at her as he spoke. She was looking at him and for a moment, he thought he might not pass out, that he might actually be able to speak to this girl.

"Not really. I've always liked the National League. I think the designated hitter rule ruins the purity of the game."

Sam could not believe what he was hearing. He had thought the exact same thing for his entire life. Pitchers are players too, they should have to hit just like every body else. They reached the teller and Sam insisted on buying the tokens. He used his birthday money which, until recently, he had planned to save for a new bat, but this would be so much more worth it.

They went to the far corner of the arcade to play a driving game. Amy was pretty good. She nearly lapped Sam the second time they played. And while he ordinarily would have been bothered by losing to someone, he could not help feeling really good. He liked watching her smile and listening to her laugh as they played.

They played until they were out of tokens and then went to find Jake, Zach and Molly, who were gathered around a game called "Zombie Invasion." Molly was kicking Jake's butt, shooting twice the zombies he was with her pink imitation pistol. Zach could hardly contain himself as Jake grew more and more frustrated. He laughed as his friend began making excuses.

"The sights are off ... You have easier shots ... This machine is nothing but a pile of junk!"

"Mine seems to be working fine," Molly chided as she blew three more zombies away.

"Do you want to go somewhere and talk?" Amy asked Sam and he jumped at the opportunity. "We'll see you guys later," he said.

"Okay, see ya,"' Molly said as Jake muttered curses under his breath.

Amy and Sam sat on the steps that used to lead to the balcony in the old Rialto days. The stairs were sort of out of the way and a little quieter than anywhere in the main part of the arcade. Sam was comfortable, but excited. He was having a great time and wanted to know everything there was to know about Amy Connor. She was born in Pittsburgh, but lived in Wisconsin, California and Cleveland before moving to Smithville three years ago. Her dad used to be a salesman and that took them all around the country. But one day he lost his job, and he and her mom decided to move to Smithville to open an organic produce business. It was a hit and they had customers all over the country – restaurants mostly. But for once they were stable and it looked like they were going to be staying in Smithville.

Amy was an only child and used to be a model, but she didn't like to make a big deal of it. She liked Smithville, but she missed Cleveland. She had a lot of friends there.

"Is that where your boyfriend is?" The words left Sam's mouth before he could do anything it.

"Boyfriend? What makes you think I have a boyfriend?"

"Uh, it's just that someone, well a girl like you has to have a boyfriend. I just figured you had one and he was some kind of genius quarterback or something." He was trying to back paddle, but knew that he was only making himself look like an idiot.

"That's very sweet of you, but I don't have a boyfriend. I never have had a boyfriend. And if I did I certainly would not have asked Molly to introduce me to you like I did."

Sam was stunned.

"You asked her to meet me?"

"Yes of course. I've been wanting to meet you since that day in the lunch room. I think you were really cool the way you stood up to Butch the way you did."

"And how did he do that Amy?" Butch put his paw on Sam's shoulder sending shivers down his back. Sam, who had nearly forgotten about Butch's threat, was all of the sudden reminded of the giant who wanted to kill him. He tried to stand up and turn around, but Butch was pushing him down on the step. Bud and Bart came into view as they corned Sam and Amy on the steps. Sam had been so stunned by Amy's revelation that he hadn't noticed them sneaking up from behind.

Butch spun Sam around laid into his shoulder with a massive fist, his middle knuckle exposed.

The pain went right into Sam's chest and up his neck, but he stood up, putting himself between the Williams's gang and Amy. He had no idea what he was going to do.

"I think we've interrupted the lovers, boys," said Butch, his voice getting deeper and meaner with every syllable. Bud and Bart nodded and grinned like two hyenas about to be given a steak. Butch cracked his knuckles and stood directly in front of Sam.

"Why don't you just leave us alone?" Amy was trying to reason with these beasts. There was no reasoning with them, Sam thought. He swallowed hard, hoping for a miracle.

"They want to be alone boys," Butch grumbled. He snorted as if he was going to savor what would come next. He put his foot on the first step as Amy and Sam backed up two more. Butch was holding the railings on both sides, his wide arms blocking any hope of escape from the front, the wood wall built to block off the former balcony was blocking off to the rear. Sam closed his eyes and tried to shield Amy. "Should we leave them alone? Or should we give City Boy what he's got coming to him."

Butch stood up as if about to pounce and Sam had the feeling that the end was near and he could die happy because he had spent time with Amy – time that she wanted to spend with him as well. He wanted to sneak one more look at her, but couldn't turn around. Butch started to take off his jacket when a loud 'thud' cracked the tense silence. Bart crumpled to his knees, revealing Zach standing there with a sock full of tokens in his hand. Butch turned to see what had happened and Sam pounced like a cornered tiger. He grabbed the railing with both hands and swung both legs forward into Butch's chest, sending the man-child hurtling through the air in a wide arc. He slammed hard against the ground and Sam grabbed Amy's hand, pulling her down the stairs just as Zach took a second swing with his sock of tokens – this one making solid contact with Bud's head, leaving all three Williams in a crumpled mass on the floor at the bottom of the steps.

The five of them – Sam, Amy, Molly, Zach and Jake – ran. They ran fast and hard, out the front door of the arcade, across Smithville Square and into the darkness toward Sam and Molly's house. Jake was cackling into the chilly night air.

"Did you see that? Did you see what we just did? Man! That was awesome!" Jake said.

"We?" Molly asked pointedly as they ran. "I didn't see you getting into it."

"I was waiting for my moment!" Jake sounded defensive. Sam was still holding Amy's hand, not wanting to let go. They ran all the way to the gravel driveway outside Sam and Molly's house and onto the front porch, where they finally stopped, bending over to catch their breath.

Sam was breathing hard with his hands on his knees and when he stood up, he was shocked to feel Amy's lips pressed against his. His head got dizzy, his stomach felt like he was on a roller coaster. She pulled away and smiled at him.

"Thank you," she said. Everyone stood there in silence as a wide grin creeped across Sam's face.

Just then the porch light went on and his mom opened the door.

"What are you kids doing here? I thought you were at the arcade."

"Um, we were," said Sam.

"Mrs. Drake!" Jake interrupted. "So lovely to see you again. We thought we might spend a little time here this evening, if that's alright."

Jake kept talking as they all went inside. Sam checked the lock on the door and the five of them went up to Sam's room. His mom promised to bring up a snack and Jake smooth-talked her into baking some cookies.

Chapter Nine

Sam's head was still swimming from Amy's kiss when they all got to his room. In his excitement, in the heat of the moment, he had forgotten that they had left the tennis ball can with the feather in it out on the bed, along with a notebook with all of their notes from their conversations about Jack Jacobs and what they planned to do next.

"What's all this stuff?" Molly asked, as Sam was staring into Amy's deep pools of blue eyes. The question brought him back to reality, if only for a moment. Jake tried to butt in.

"Oh that's nothing. It's nothing, my fair Molly," he tried to snatch the feather out of her hand, but Zach slapped his hand away and handed it to her gently.

Molly turned away from Jake and examined the feather. Amy joined her near the desk, leaving the three boys huddling near the bed.

"We should not tell them anything," said Jake. "No offense, Sam, but I don't trust your sister."

Zach slapped him on the back of the head with a 'you're a moron' expression, then turned to Sam as if leaving the decision about whether or not to tell them up to him.

"We should tell them," Sam said, then turning to Jake, "They might be able to help us."

The boys told Amy and Molly everything – from Jack's brother through the night they watched the movie to how they have been planning to follow Jack into the woods.

"Is that why you didn't want to go hiking this weekend?" Molly asked Sam, busting her brother in a lie.

"Yeah."

"This can't be true," she said. "None of this is possible." She hoped Amy would support her, but instead her friend stayed quiet, silently acknowledging she believed what the boys had said. They all stared silently at the feather for a moment, the image of an eighth-grader being carried off burned clearly in the front of their minds.

Just then, there was a knock on the door. Sam jumped, worried that the Williams gang had shown up. Jake touched his arm to calm him, then walked to the door and opened it.

"Mrs. Drake! Thank you so much for providing nourishment. Please, please come in."

Molly, who was still holding the feather hid it behind her back and the four of them lined up in a perfect line as mom brought the snacks in to the room.

"Are you kids okay? You look like you've seen a ghost."

"Nope. Nope, we're fine. Thanks for asking. Just some good natured chatting, that's all." Jake escorted Molly's mom to the door, thanking her again for her 'hallmark hospitality' once again before closing the door behind her.

The boys had a plan. Well, they sort of did anyway. They planned to wait until spring break, which was just a couple of weeks away, then follow Jack into the woods. They would tell their parents they were camping out at each others' houses and take provisions for up to two nights. They'd follow Jack until they understood better what it was he was doing in the woods. That's when they would confront him.

"Then what?" Amy asked.

"What?" said Sam.

"Well, once you have him in the woods and you starting talking to him, then what are you going to do."

"Nothing," said Jake. "We're just going to talk to him."

"Why not just talk to him at school?" Molly was joining her friend in skepticism.

"Because, Molly," Jake said. "We can't be sure what he's up to if we talk to him at school."

"Well are you going to help him look for the body?" The thought sent a shiver down Sam's back, but he supposed that's exactly what they were going to do. And if they found it? He wasn't quite sure. But maybe they would get a look at the beast responsible for the conversion of Jack Jacobs. Maybe, just maybe, they could help to bring it to justice. If nothing else, they would know for sure what lurked in the woods of the State Park outside of town.

"We're in," Amy said confidently.

"You're what?" asked Jacob.

"We're in," said Molly. "We want to help you."

"I don't think so," Jake protested. "This is our plan and certainly too dangerous for a couple of girls. Isn't that right Sam?"

Sam was lost in Amy's eyes, and when he looked at Molly he recognized that look she gave him when she was not going to be swayed.

"It's fine with me," he said. Jake was furious. He tried to stammer out how they could not be helpful and would only slow the three boys down, but his protests were met with muted contempt. He finally resigned himself to the fact that the three boys were going to have company and this trio of intrepid adventurers had just become a quintet. The question was what to do next?

The five of them sat huddled on the floor of Sam's room, going over the facts, making plans and talking about the possibilities of what might happen the day they follow Jack Jacobs into the woods.

Chapter Ten

The next week at school, none of them could concentrate on anything but the plan. Amy and Molly started eating lunch in the perch with the boys, a change Sam welcomed. He loved spending every second possible with Amy and he thought she might feel the same way. They agreed to not speak about the plan while in school, instead saving these discussions for daily meetings in Jake and Zach's tree fort after the final bell. What they did talk about were Jack sightings.

Each of them kept their eyes peeled during the day to try and spot their elusive trophy, reporting back to the rest of the group during lunch. Amy and Zach had a class with him, Jake usually saw him in the hall after wood shop. Sam and Molly had no scheduled meetings with Jack, but each tried to vary their schedule and class routines a little each day to catch a glimpse of him.

"So what do we know?" asked Sam as he ignored his bowl of beef vegetable soup.

"I've never seen him go to his locker," Amy said.

"Yeah, it's almost like he doesn't use it or something," added Jake.

This surveillance, this team spying on Jack, was yielding very little useful information. So far all they knew was that he had fourth period history with Amy and Zach and never showed up for lunch. He was out the door almost before the final bell had finished ringing and off into the woods.Trying to figure out Jack's schedule was proving pointless since he didn't seem to have one. They decided it might be best to consider the other things they knew.

That afternoon, the five of them met in the tree house for more discussion and planning. Sam brought the feather and the notebook, Jake brought snacks.

"Not all treasures are gold," Molly repeated to herself. "What does that mean? I mean, if he's writing things like that on the bathroom wall, then its almost like he wants some one to know what he's up to."

"Yeah, its like he's on a treasure hunt," Amy said, "But the treasure isn't gold, its his brother's body."

It was a disgusting thought, and for a moment each of them pondered privately what exactly they were getting themselves into. Were they really going to follow a boy into the woods only to possibly discover a deadly beast and bones of a boy only a year older than they were?

Though they all thought it, none of them spoke of their reservations. Instead they finalized the plan.

Spring break was a week away. They would use the spring dance as the launch point for their plot. Sam and Molly would tell their mom they were going to the dance and that they were going to spend the night at Jake's and Amy's houses. Jake would tell his mom he was spending the night at Zach's and Amy would say she was going to spend the night at Molly's.

Since Zach's parents were going to be out of town, he didn't have to tell them anything. But Mrs. Drake was going to be a chaperone at the dance, so they all had to go. They would leave their camping equipment at Zach's house and head back there after the dance. If their guess was right, Jack Jacobs would be heading into the woods sometime early Saturday morning, so they could spend the night in the tree house and wait for him there. Then, they'd follow him at a distance until he stopped – and then they'd confront him.

It sounded simple and they all knew what they had to do, yet there was a certain anxiety they all felt about the whole thing. It was part excitement, part fear, part wonder. No matter what, they decided, they would not split up, even if it meant abandoning their cause.

The days of the final week before spring break went by slowly, like yogurt pouring from a glass. Thank goodness they didn't have tests, because as distracted as they all were, they probably would have failed. Finally, Friday came and after school they all went home to pack their bags and get ready for the dance.

Chapter Eleven

Sam had been to dances before, when he was in sixth grade. He had looked forward to the winter dance at his old school, but the family had moved before it took place. It used to be that he went to dances to spend time with his friends – to goof around and have a good time. There was never a particular reason, or girl, that ever made him want to go before. Rather, it was just that going to dances was the thing to do on a Friday night. This dance was different, for a lot of reasons. While he was nervous about what was going to happen the next day, he was excited to see Amy. He wondered what she would wear, whether or not they would dance to every song or just every once in a while.

He hoped he knew how to dance.

"It can't be that hard, right?" he asked, trying to adjust his hair in the hallway mirror.

"I'm sure you'll be fine," Molly said. Sam noticed that his sister was dressed up. He could not remember the last time he saw her wear a dress – Easter maybe. She looked pretty, he thought, even if it was his sister.

"Who are you all dressed up for?" he asked.

"Oh, no one in particular," she said coyly, before turning and heading down the stairs.

Sam and Molly had stashed their camping gear at Zach's house after school, so as not to raise their mom's suspicion when she took them to the dance. They both packed overnight bags, though there was nothing really in them. Sam's had his baseball glove and a sweatshirt in it; Molly's was nothing but her gym clothes and a couple of books.

"Don't you two look nice!" Mom was waiting at the bottom of the stairs. "I have got to get a picture of my babies all grown up and on their way to the dance."

"Aw mom!" Sam protested. Molly shot him a look as if to say 'Shut your mouth and do what she wants. We don't want to upset her now do we?'

"I wish your dad could be here for this, he was so sorry he had to go out of town."

Sam thought that his dad not being around was actually better; that way there was very little chance he would have to come home early the next morning to do chores or go to the store or anything.

"Its okay," Molly said, putting her bag down to pose for the obligatory photos.

After what felt to Sam to be hours of photos, they were finally on their way. The dance was in the cafeteria, which had been decorated to look like a forest. The theme, The Darling Buds of Spring, was the dance committee' s idea. Sam didn't get it. He thought it should have been something like Rock 'til you Drop or Dances Stink, but This One Will Be Cool Since Amy will Be There. Too wordy, maybe.

When they arrived, Molly went off to find Amy and some other friends, while Sam made his way to where he told Jake and Zach to meet him – in the jock comer. Hopefully he could remain low, dance with Amy and sneak off without incident. Mom took her place in the perch with Mr. Hutson and couple of other parents Sam didn't know.

Everyone was dressed up, even the geeks and Future Farmers of America – who were topped out in their best overalls and white shirts. The dance floor was crowded and the room felt like an ocean, full and swaying in rhythmic waves. It was dark, mostly, except for the strobe lights and lights near the doorways. Sam was shoving his way through the crowd, as politely as he could. He caught a glimpse of Jake – who appeared to be trying to tell him something, but the music was too loud, he could not hear it.

Sam never saw it coming, the blinding flash and sudden upward rush of the ground. He must have blacked out for a second, because the next thing he knew he was on the ground, a thick stream of metallic tasting blood streaming down the back of his throat. The room was spinning around him, when suddenly the lights went on. Above him were familiar faces – Jake, Zach, Molly, his mom. His eyes came to focus on Amy, who had never looked prettier. Her hair was back, off of her face and she was wearing a silver dress that reminded Sam of angels' wings.

Each time he closed his eyes he felt the room pulse, as if he were in some sort of giant lung, fluctuating with every breath. The music had stopped and the room – which was still full of students – was oddly silently, except for the sound of Mr. Hutson's voice booming.

"Williams! That is it! I have had it with you and all of your crap!"

Sam felt his shoulders being pulled off the ground and his head coming to rest in his mom's lap.

She was crying.

"Sam! Sam! Are you alright baby?"

He looked back at Amy and smiled. He nodded his head as best as he could, but it felt heavy. He could feel the blood coming from his nose now. Jake disappeared and came back with some tissues. Amy knelt down to hold his hand.

Soon Mr. Hutson was at his side. He held a can of cold pop on the bridge of Sam's nose and it felt like an iceberg, heavy and incredibly cold.

"Now don't worry Mrs. Drake. He'll be okay," he heard the principal say. Sam looked at Amy, who had a tear coming down the side of her face. Molly was crying too and Jake kept saying, "Sam, are you okay buddy?"

Zach, who had said maybe three words the entire time Sam had known him, looked angry. He was muttering between his gritted teeth. "Dirty pig-licker. Sucker punch my friend. Boy I can't wait to get him alone in a dark place."

"Zach that's enough," Mr. Hutson said. "Mrs. Drake, I think he'll be okay, but we might want to call an ambulance."

Sam suddenly realized that he had not said anything. All of the sudden, everything became perfectly clear. Going to the hospital meant not staying at the dance. Not staying at the dance meant not going to Zach's. Not going to the Zach's meant not following Jack Jacobs into the woods.

"No!" he said. Everyone's eyes snapped to Sam's face and the pain hit him like a ton of bricks, as if Butch had just socked him again. "I mean, no, I'm fine. I want to stay."

Mrs. Drake tried to protest, but he wouldn't let her.

"Just get him and his cousins out of here," said Sam. "I'll be okay, seriously, mom, I'll be fine. Just please let me stay."

Mr. Hutson and his mom finally agreed to let Sam stay at the dance and, once the Williams gang was escorted out of the building by Mr. Hutson, the dance was free to resume. Mrs. Drake helped Sam get cleaned up. His nose hurt and there was blood all over his white shirt, but other than that he was okay. Molly went to his locker and retrieved his gym shirt. He told his mom he wanted to keep his ruined Sunday shirt. He tried to smile as much as possible. It hurt to smile, it hurt a lot, but he had to put on a good enough show that his mom would let him stay.

The dance was nearly half over by the time he made it to the dance floor. Amy, Molly, Jake and Zach were standing in the comer, not dancing, not talking.

"What's the matter with all of you? Haven't you ever seen a guy take a punch before?" They all sort of smiled when he came up to them. They were glad he was alright. Molly grabbed his hand and squeezed. He put his arm around her. "Don't worry sis, I'm fine."

"That was awesome" Jake said. "No offense. I tried to warn you ..."

He kept talking as Sam looked at Zach. His silent friend gave Sam a knowing nod, like, sorry I missed that one, but next time I got your back. Sam now realized just how tough Zach really was.

Amy looked at Sam as if he might just break. He tried to smile, but managed only a grin – his nose hurt too badly. She rushed to him and threw her arms around his neck. They began to sway with the music and Sam realized he was finally dancing, dancing with the girl of his dreams, dancing with Amy. They began to twirl slowly to the rhythm of the song and Sam looked up to the perch to see his mom standing there with tears in her eyes, an expression of pride on her face. Her baby was all grown up.

The rest of the dance went on without incident. Sam and Amy danced every slow dance and Jake showed off what he believed were tremendous break dancing skills. It was the calm before the storm they all expected the next day and they enjoyed it. Sam went to the bathroom every three or four songs to make sure that his nose was not bleeding and every time he felt like he was becoming increasingly deformed.

His nose was swollen and looked a little crooked. The color was funny too, like a purple and red sunset. It hurt. A lot. But he was oddly pleased with himself, like he was some kind of warrior. He had survived what Butch had dished out and he was not scared anymore. Plus, he got the girl. He was pleased indeed.

Mrs. Drake watched carefully from the perch and came down a couple of times to check on Sam.

"You really need to ice this," she said. "Make sure you put ice on it when you get to Zach's house and call me if it starts to hurt to bad."

Sam could tell she was worried. He knew she was worried and she wanted him to go home after the last song. She probably wanted to make him a snack and put him into bed, but he had to resist. He had to make sure he could continue with the plan. He tried to be adult about the whole thing.

"Mom, I appreciate that you're worried, but I'll be fine." He gave her a hug and let her kiss him on the cheek. Ordinarily this would have been tremendously embarrassing- letting your mommy give you a kiss in front of the whole school? Quelle nightmare! But he had bigger fish to fry, and its not like he was the king of the school to start off with.

The lights in the cafeteria went on after the DJ played the last song – a nice slow, long one that Sam savored every moment of. He suddenly loved to dance, but the bright florescence of the overhead lighting was a wake-up call. Back to reality. Back to the plan at hand. Sam turned from Amy and noticed that Molly had danced the last dance with Zach while Jake hovered around the punch bowl, waiting for the song to end.

Chapter Twelve

Sam's face felt like it had been crushed by a giant bolder and run over by car when Zach shook him awake the next morning. In fact, his whole body hurt from sleeping on the uneven wood floor of the tree house. It was early, very early. The sun was just coming up and the five of them were all groggy from a lack of sleep. Molly was cold and Jake, who normally ran his mouth non-stop, was quiet. Zach was the only one who seemed to be perfectly alert. He opened the windows as the rest of them rubbed the sleep from their eyes and stretched.

"Oh gosh, your nose!" Molly shrieked.

"Yeah, Sam, that looks awful," added Jake.

"Great," said Sam, gently touching his swollen beak, "It looks as bad as it feels."

Amy opened up her backpack, took out a handful of granola bars and passed them around. They all began to eat and groan with aches and pains.

"I think I slept on a nail. Who built this thing anyway?" Molly griped. "It obviously was not designed to be sleeping quarters."

Zach shushed her and made a motion with his hand for all of them to get down and stay quiet. He had seen something in the woods, making its way to the clearing outside the tree house window. It was Jack Jacobs. They all tried not to make a sound while Zach tilted his head to peer over the edge with one eye.

Jack came into the clearing and continued across it with his back to the tree house. There was an opening in the trees across the way and he went straight for it. The opening was the start of a trail that lead to the State Park a couple miles away. They waited for Zach to give the okay, then rushed to pack up their bags. They didn't want to follow too close behind Jack, but they didn't want to let him get too far ahead either. If they lost him, this was all for nothing. So one-by-one they descended the make-shift ladder – pieces of two-by-four hammered into the side of the tree – and when they were all down they started off after the boy with the red back pack.

At first, their pace was brisk. They stayed in a single-file line, each being careful to not step on fallen branches or anything else that might make a loud noise. They didn't really know how far ahead Jack might be so they wanted to be careful. The trail here was flat and relatively straight, making it an easy hike, more of a walk really. They covered the first mile without incident and each felt their aches and pains dissolving as their muscles warmed up and the morning sun climbed higher into the sky.

By 9:30 they reached Highway 32 and as they approached the opening in the trees, they paused while Zach went ahead to try and see Jack. He spotted him across the highway, on the other side of four lanes and median, disappearing into the trees beyond.

"The trail must pick up on the other side," Sam noted and they all concurred. They waited for a break in the traffic and ran across the first two lanes into the median where they ducked into a ditch. Jake, who had sense enough to bring the binoculars his dad used for bird watching, creeped to the rim to make sure the coast was clear. There was a break in the trees and a short wooden pillar with a white diamond on it indicating the continuation of a trail.

"The coast is clear."

They jumped up and sprinted across the two lanes of traffic, down the berm and into the trees, where they stopped a moment to catch their breath before continuing with their silent, single-file march. The trees were denser on this side of the road, and taller. Everywhere they looked were shadows, and it felt a little cooler – though they had all taken off their coats and stowed them. There was a sign next to the trail about a hundreds yards in:

Smithville State Park White Diamond Trail: No Hunting. No Open Flames.

It didn't take long for the trail to become more challenging. It narrowed and started to climb, and unlike the other side of the highway – which was well-manicured – it was mostly dirt and mud. There were no wood chips to cushion their steps and rocks made it hard to get into a rhythm.

Sam was breathing hard as the trail wound up the hill. He couldn't see the top, making it hard to understand what they were climbing toward. He wondered if they would ever make it to the top, let alone to a stretch of trail that actually went down. Beads of sweat were falling from his face and when he went to wipe them away, he accidentally bumped his nose – causing it to start bleed in a slight but steady stream. He wiped the blood off his face as he walked and picked a handful of leaves off the ground next to the trail to wipe them off. They were old, from last fall's shedding and the blood came off his hands onto them like paint. Surely they were falling behind, there was no way they were keeping up with Jack, who Sam reasoned probably made this trip every day.

Up ahead, Zach lead the way, staying just within sight of the rest of the group. Sam had just managed to stop the flow of blood from his nose when he noticed that Zach had stopped ahead on the trail and was waiting for the rest of the group.

"What's going on?" Amy asked. "Why have we stopped?"

Zach was staring ahead and had a lost look on his face. There was a fork in the trail. To one side, the path turned almost straight up the hill. To the other, it went ahead straight around the side of the hill. They were at an impasse. Both trails disappeared relatively quickly, making it impossible to see where Jack was. Jake tried his binoculars, but could not see anything. They tried to see if footprints could guide them down one path or the other and, after several minutes of looking and pondering, they finally decided that if they were ever going to catch Jack, they needed to split.

Jake, Zach and Molly took the path up the hill, leaving Amy and Sam to explore the one that went more or less straight ahead. They watched as the other three started up the hill.

Molly was telling Jake to hurry. He was telling her to go ahead and take the lead if she was so sure that she could go faster. Zach took the lead to quiet them both down.

"How's your nose?" Amy asked as they started to walk.

"Oh, its fine," said Sam, lying just a little bit. "How are you holding up?"

"Fine, but I have to say that I'm a little nervous."

"Why?"

"Because, what if we do find him? I almost hope that we don't. It could be too scary."

Sam wanted to agree, but he wanted to appear strong at the same time, so he grunted a little and they continued to walk. They must have gone about a half-mile, maybe more, when Sam started to feel tingly. The hair on the back of his neck stood up almost straight and felt a chill running down his spine. The woods were pretty thick on either side of the trail, with heavy underbrush making it hard to see more than ten or fifteen feet to the left or right. Amy was in the lead, but for reasons he didn't quite understand, Sam had the strangest feeling that there was someone watching them. He could not have know how right he was.

Chapter Thirteen

The feeling that they were being watched followed Sam like his own shadow. He was afraid to to turn around and look, and didn't want to tell Amy that he suspected anything. They kept a brisk pace on the relatively flat trail and Sam could see light ahead. Maybe the trail ended or there was a clearing. He could not quite tell. All he knew was that more sunshine was getting through up there. He wanted to be there, he wanted to be in the sun and fast.

As they neared the light, Sam could hear noises, like people talking – shouting really – and motors, big ones, chugging away up ahead. He was too focused on the sounds ahead to hear the ones coming from behind him – branches snapping and loud footsteps – until it was too late.

He didn't have time to warn Amy. He hardly had time to breath when suddenly something dark and scratchy was thrown over his head and he was pulled backward, off his feet. He was being dragged away. Something smelled inside the bag and Sam felt his head getting light, like the time he built a model in his old bedroom without opening his window. Soon, the world was black and Sam was no longer aware of where he was or what he was doing.

A breath of cold air shot Sam's eyes open, at least he thought they were open. He couldn't see anything. There was something on his head and when he went to take it off, he realized that his arms were tied behind his back. He was lying down on what felt like rock, stone. He was cold and he could feel the damp under his fingers.

"Hello? Hello? Is anyone there? Help?" Sam's voice seemed to echo.

"Sam? Sam is that you? Where are you?"

"Amy?" a third voice chimed in. Sam recognized this one as Jakes.

"Where are we?" Sam asked and as he did, he heard a muffled groan off to his left somewhere.

"I'll tell you where we are," said Molly, "We're in trouble."

"Is anyone hurt?" Zach sounded authoritative.

"No, not really," the other four answered.

"How? What? What's going on here?" asked Amy.

"Yah, where are we? Can anyone see?" Molly asked.

Zach shushed them and they all fell silent. Fear crept over Sam like an ocean of warm syrup. He tried to remain perfectly still, shortening his breath in order to keep the noise level down. He heard shuffling, then the piercing screech of a hawk and the sound of wings shuffling as the bird came to a landing on the ground. That's it, Sam thought, I'm dead. We're all dead. The man-bird is here and he's going to eat each on of us for a snack. We're finished. He started to wish his mom had taken him home that night. He really wished they had never left Chicago. But then he thought of Amy and all the thinking made his head start to hurt.

It felt like a year before they heard another noise – though it was probably about 15 seconds. This time it was a thump, like something had just been dropped on the hard stone ground.

"Nathan, they're awake!" It was a boy's voice. "Don't just stand there help me get these masks off and untie their arms and legs."

Sam's hood was tom off and when his eyes adjusted – to the light streaming into them from the mouth of what appeared to be a cave – he focused on a face unlike any he had ever seen. It was a man, an older man and he had long gray and black hair and a beard that seemed to go from just under his eyes to the middle of his chest. He was staring at Sam with steel blue eyes from behind strands of his mop-like hair. The man smiled, revealing a twisted knot of yellow teeth. Sam could not help but gulp. His hands went slack as the rope that had them tied up was cut from behind. Appearing next to the man with the beard was a boy with blonde curly hair. It was Jack Jacobs.

"Hi," said Jack, who then turned to the other side of the chamber. "Zach, Jake, Amy. Are you guys alright?"

The room was big and relatively dark, except for the bright sunlight streaming in from one end. Jake, Zach, Amy, Molly and Sam were situated around a fire pit in the middle of the room. They had all been lying on the stone floor, which had moss on it in some parts. They all sat up when Jack cut the ropes around their hands and feet. Zach stood up and looked like he might punch Jack in the mouth, but Jake stopped him.

"Nathan, I told you to bring them here and wait for me," Jack barked. "You didn't have to scare the life out of them."

"Sorry about that Jack, but they were all getting a little close to the slide. I had to stop them or else they might have been found. Who knows what would have happened to them then."

The old man, Nathan, went toward the opening of the cave and pulled a piece of bread from Jack's red backpack. That's when Sam saw it: the biggest bird he had ever seen up close. It had to have been two feet tall, standing on a small rock near the cave opening. It's feathers were red and brown and gray, with white tips on the ends of the wings. This was the source of Sam's mysterious feather. Nathan tore a piece of the bread off and hand-fed the monstrous bird, its hooked beak nipping slightly on the old man's fingers as it took the whole wheat bread down.

Sam was confused. Someone was going to have to explain all of this and soon.

The bird's name was Nestor and it was a red-tailed hawk, a species common to this part of the state at one time, Jack explained. Nestor was Nathan's pet. Well, not pet exactly, more like his best friend. They lived in the woods, both of them. Nestor lived in the tops of the tallest trees and Nathan lived right there in the cave they were in, high on a hill off the main trail in the Smithville State Park. They were both Jack's friends.

"Whoa, what happened to your nose?" Jack asked. It was the first time he had spoken directly to Sam.

"Huh?" Sam was taken back by the question. It seemed odd, out of place. He was thinking about the feather and the message and Jake's story about the Bird-Man and Craig. He had forgotten about his bloody, pulsing nose. "Oh, nothing. I took a punch, that's all. What happened to the Bird-Man that ate your brother?"

Jack's face crunched together like had just seen trigonometry for the very first time. He titled his head as if to ask 'Bird-Man?'

"You know," Sam continued, "You and your brother were hiking up here and this half-bird, half-man thing carried your brother off and nearly got you. Then you got all weird and stuff. The Bird-Man!"

"I don't know anything about a Bird-Man," Jack said. He was beginning to think that maybe the punch had knocked a couple of boards loose in Sam's head.

"Everyone knows the story," said Jake who was jumping in part to protect Sam and also to get answers.

"Yeah, you and your brother came up here for a hike and you fell behind?" Molly hoped Jack would take the story from there, but he said nothing. "You fell behind and when you caught up this wicked beast had your brother in its talons and carried it off into the woods."

Jack sat down on a stone and pondered what they were saying. He thought long and hard about how to bridge the gap between their story and what he knew to be true about his brother.

"My brother and I haven't been hiking up here since the summer before sixth grade," Jack started. The others hung on his every word, they were nodding as if they knew that part. They wanted details. They wanted to hear about the beast and his constant search to find the decrepit remains of his big brother Craig. "Right before my parents got divorced and he went to live with my dad in Boston."

What? Divorced? Boston? That's it? They felt like they had seen a magic trick and then had the magician explain that there was no magic to it at all. Or like they just found out there was no Easter Bunny.

"Divorced?" asked Jake enraged. "Boston?"

"What do you mean he lives with your dad?" Amy tagged in.

"My parents got divorced and my brother wanted to go to this private school in Boston, so he moved up there with my dad. What on Earth made you think that he was eaten?"

All eyes turned to Jake, who shrugged his shoulders and made a defensive looking face.
"Hey," he said, "That's the story I was told."

Zach punched him in the arm as the others groaned.

"So, if you haven't been up here every day looking for your brother's corpse, what are you doing up here?" Molly asked for the rest of the group.

They all waited for his answer.

Chapter Fourteen

Jack was more than a little surprised to learn of the rumors that had been following his behavior change. The divorce was hard on him and he missed Craig. They got to see each other on holidays and for a week or two over the summer. It was easier for Jack to visit Boston, so his brother never came back. Craig had just sort of disappeared, but not at the hands – or talons – of some mythical woods beast. It was worse than that. He had disappeared because of divorce and distance.

Jack thought about how to begin explaining everything he had been up to. He sat down near the opening of the cave, where Nathan was sitting with his hands on his knees, Nestor resting stately upon his leather-clad forearm. He would start with Nathan. Hopefully that would clear things up.

"I met Nathan the last time Craig and I came up here hiking," Jack said. It was just before his dad and brother moved off to Boston. Craig brought Jack up here to show him around the woods, to spend some time together before having to say goodbye. They had been walking along the trail – much like Sam, Amy, Molly, Jake and Zach had been – when they heard the same kinds of noises Sam had. It sounded like machines. And people talking. They were almost to the place where the noises were coming from when they heard Nestor screech from the trees above them. Nathan grabbed them, putting his hands over their mouths and pulling them back into the woods. They were afraid at first. Craig was ready to fight and Jack was hoping his big brother could protect them both. But Nathan explained that he was not trying to hurt them, but save them. Those noises and the people making them were very dangerous.

Nathan looked like an old man, but he was only twenty-eight. He used to work for an advertising company, writing television commercials and running errands, but his real passion was in the outdoors. Two years ago, he decided to take a hike in the Smithville State Park. He packed his backpack in his car and set out for what was supposed to have been a three day adventure, then he would go back to work the following Monday and dream about other places to visit. He liked to hike alone. He liked the feeling
of being alone in the wilderness – listening to the sounds of the birds and the trees, taking in the sights and smells. He loved to talk to other hikers as they crossed paths somewhere deep in the woods.

On his second day hiking in Smithville, Nathan was enjoying an early morning jaunt along the trail that lead to Parrish Peak when he heard something out of place. It was metallic, like a machine. He was used to the loud chirps of morning doves and robins, the rustling of the trees and the bubbling of the creek, so this sound stuck out like a sore thumb. It was distant, but distinct, clear among the trees and animals, which had fallen silent leaving only this thump, thump, and buzz. Curious, Nathan decided to hike until he found the source of the racket. As came over a ridge, the sound became louder and louder until he saw something that changed his life forever.

Smithville State Park is enormous and vastly understaffed. There were only three rangers stationed to patrol an area roughly the size of Los Angeles. Because it was a state park, it was supposed to be protected from things like hunting and logging. But when Nathan crossed the top of the ridge that day, he saw that the laws protecting the trees and animals of Smithville State Park were not being enforced very well. Down in the valley below the ridge were two huge swaths of barren, dead ground. Stumps marked the places where trees had been like headstones in a cemetery.

Standing alone on the barren ridge, Nathan watched as two crews of five men chopped at old-growth sycamore and pine trees with axes and chainsaws. He felt as if someone had just punched him in the stomach, taking his breath away. He was stunned for a moment, until he realized the chopping and sawing had stopped. He had been spotted and the men were now running up the hill after him.

Nathan ran.

He ambled back down the trail that took him to the ridge. He managed to get back into the trees just as the men were coming over the top of the hill. He felt his heart stop as the sound of a gunshot rang out and the bark of a tree to his left burst into splinters and sawdust. They were shooting at him! He ran as fast as his feet would carry him, faster than what he thought was safe, and he nearly fell a couple of times as the slope of the trail grew steeper and steeper. He cut off the trail and into the woods, weaving among the trees and hopping over fallen ones. Soon all he heard was the sound of his own breath and his heart pumping. He looked behind him to see if the men were coming and could see movement back in the direction of the trail.

Nathan doubled back so he was heading back up the hill, but he stayed away from the trail. He found the entrance to a cave and quickly ducked inside. He had left most of his gear at his campsite, but did have his binoculars in his backpack. He laid down on the ground and tried to scope the men from his perch. He saw them as they ran down the trail. There were six of them. One was carrying a gun. They ran past him in the direction of his campsite. Nathan stayed close to the ground in the cave and tried to slow down his breath. He needed to get out of the park, to find a ranger and tell them about the logging and the men chasing him. He needed to tell someone that he had been shot at. But Nathan was afraid. He didn't know how to get out from where he was. He didn't know if it would be safe.

So he waited. He waited for two days in that cave, alone, with no food or blankets. He only had a little water in a bottle. He made it last as long as he could. As the sun set on the third day, Nathan decided to make a move. If he didn't, he knew he would either starve or freeze to death. The nights were getting colder.

Nathan made his way back to his campsite, down the trail from his haven in the cave. His body hurt from sitting and sleeping on the hard cave floor. It was dark by the time he got there, but he didn't need a lot of light to see what had happened. His tent was tom to shreds and the stuffing from his sleeping back was spread across the ground like confetti. All of his food had been dumped out and picked over by animals. Even his spare socks were tom to shreds. It had to have been the men, he thought. It had to have been the loggers who did this. He rummaged through what was left of his belongings and found his cell phone shattered to pieces, his map torn to shreds. His rain jacket, which he had left behind on the morning of his exploratory hike, was still intact, as was his first-aid kit, which contained matches. Nathan was a good 14 miles from the nearest road and almost double that from a ranger station. Of course he had no way of knowing how far it was without a map and no way of which direction to go since his compass was laying in pieces at his feet.

"What did he do?" Jake blurted out. It was the first interruption in Jack's story. "Hang on and I'll tell you," he continued.

Nathan could not make it out of the park the way he came, not at night anyway, so he decided to climb back up to the ridge. With any luck the loggers would be gone and maybe there would be an access road that would lead him out. They had to have been hauling the logs away somehow. His body ached and his stomach groaned, but Nathan made his way up the hill in the dark. Once he got past the tree line, he ducked down and watched for a while, letting his eyes adjust to the faint moonlight and making sure there was no one around. Higher and higher he crept, getting closer with every hesitant step to the ridge, the same ridge where one of the men was standing when they tried to kill him!

The ridge was like a lunar landscape – craggy rock and no vegetation. The dim glow of the moon made everything appear blue. As he neared the top of the ridge, Nathan got down on his belly and crawled, like a soldier ducking below enemy sight. He peered over the edge and realized he was close to where he had been a few days before. Even in the dark, the sight was overwhelming. Two barren swaths, wider than a football field is long, cut down the hill into the valley like brushstrokes. He felt shocked and angry and hurt, much the same way he had when his neighbor accidentally ran over his dog the year before. Only this was no accident.

He watched carefully for headlights or flashlights, and listened for the sound of motors or axes or people talking. After a few minutes of scanning the valley, Nathan thought it was safe to stand. He did so and walked along the ridge looking at the devastation below. When he reached a point that he was above where trees still stood, he turned down the hill and began his descent into the valley. He moved carefully, fighting gravity and fatigue to keep a slow but steady pace as he descended. And when he came to the tree line, he peered in for a moment before taking a step. There was no trail here. He would have to find his way down through the trees, in the dark and alone.

Nathan figured he must have been half-way down the valley when he stopped to take a rest. His thighs were burning and he was thirsty from the exertion. He leaned against a tree and that's when he saw it, the body. It looked like it had been shot. One side was blown out and bloody, and there were maggots crawling from the wound. He knew it was a hawk and given Smithville's location in the world, probably a red-tailed hawk. It was dead. Very dead. He knew the loggers had done this. And it was pointless. He was ready to keep moving, his anger seething – when he heard it. The small voice, chirping, cheeping, begging for help. In the tree above him, Nathan made out the silhouette of a nest. That's where the sound was coming from. Though he was exhausted and drained of strength, Nathan climbed up the tree to find a single hatchling. Right away he knew from the shape of the beak that it was a red-tailed.

The broken carcass at the base of the tree must have been its mother. He wondered how long it had been up in the nest alone. He wondered how much longer the baby hawk would last without food. He had to do something.

Nathan called the baby bird Nestor and did the best he could to build a little nest inside his backpack while balancing on the tree limbs. He piled sticks and leaves on top of his jacket and zipped the baby bird up while he climbed down the tree.

Nathan fed Nestor berries from bushes in the underbrush and took some for himself, hoping they were not poisonous. It took nearly two hours to make it all the way to the valley floor, but when he did Nathan was relieved to find a dirt road. Relieved and saddened. He decided to head to the right, which he assumed would be east toward Smithville. A few hundred yards down the road he came across some machinery – trucks, trailers, a bulldozer and what looked like a crane. Nathan was furious. This was the equipment belonging to the loggers. These were the people who had tried to kill him and succeeded in killing Nestor's mother. This was now his enemy. Though weak, he decided to take action, cutting the stems off all the tires on the trucks and trailers. He put dirt in the gas tanks of the heavy equipment and drained the fuel from the smaller machinery. It was small revenge, but revenge none the less.

Dawn would be coming soon, so Nathan moved as quickly as he could along the road – careful not to hurt Nestor. He hoped to not be around when the loggers came in the morning. He hoped to make it out of the woods alive.

When he reached the edge of the state park, Nathan thought first about going to the Ranger Station. It was built like a log cabin and housed some offices, but mostly a store that sold all kids of camping, hiking and fishing gear. There was no one inside. He waited for a few minutes, then decided to set off up the highway to find his car. He would go to the police, he thought. But the police said they didn't have jurisdiction in the park. The rangers would have to handle the investigation. The officer behind the desk at the station said he would try to contact the rangers and gave Nathan directions to find the station. and instructions to head straight there.

He was pulling up to the ranger station when he saw one of the trucks from the night before – one of the one's he had flattened the tires on. A ranger was standing outside, speaking with another man.

Nathan assumed he was the driver. The two men were talking and laughing. They must be friends. So much for the rangers helping out, he thought. He pulled past the Ranger Station without stopping and hoped he would not be recognized.

Just then, Nestor began chirping from the passenger seat of Nathan' s small car. He had planned on leaving the bird with the rangers. They would take care of him, he reasoned. But after seeing the ranger talking to the man from the logging company, he knew the rangers could not be trusted.

Nathan could have pulled away right then. He could have kept driving and made it home by dinner. He could have gone to work the next day and explained to his boss why he missed a couple of days work. The trip lasted longer than expected. He had car trouble. Nathan could have thought of a million different excuses. But he didn't. At that moment, Nathan knew he had a decision to make. He could pull away, maybe leaving Nestor with an animal shelter a few counties away. He could leave the Smithville State Park to be ravaged by illegal logging. Or he could choose to stay and fight. Images of the painted swaths of barren earth and Nestor's mother flashed through his brain. He thought about the loggers and their willingness to kill him for discovering the truth. He thought about these things and his heart began to swell with anger and sadness, his mind cleared like a fan blowing smoke out of a small room. He was determined. He would save these woods and the animals that called it home. He would save the woods for the animals and for people like him who wanted to enjoy the outdoors. He would save them for future generations. He would save them for Nestor. He would save them for himself.

Chapter Fifteen

Sam was amazed by what he had just heard. Jack's story about Nathan seemed almost impossible. He had a hard time believing any of it. A homeless hiker lives in a cave and saves birds? And what about these loggers? How could they possibly get away with stripping a state park clean of trees? Wouldn't somebody notice? It seemed that they were all trying to take in Jack's story. Even Jake, who usually responded to just about any emotion with words, had fallen silent. Nestor was nibbling bits of cracker from Nathan's hand and Jack sat there on his rock, not moving. He looked at them like he had just revealed the truth about Santa Clause – waiting for a response, hoping one of them would pose a question, say something, grunt. Instead they all just sat there, silently. The only noise in the cave was the slight clip of Nestor's beak and the wind in the trees outside.

Sam wanted to say something. He wanted to ask a question, but he could not come up with one. He looked at Amy who was wearing a stunned expression. As was Molly. Jake was looking out the entrance to the cave and Zach stared at the floor. The silence was deafening. It felt like no one had spoken for hours – though it had probably only been a minute or so since Jack finished his story. Molly was the first to break the silence.

"So ... so," she stammered, "he's been living up here for two years? In a cave with a pet hawk?"

"Yeah," Jack said as matter-of-factly as if he had just been asked if he was sure that he wanted to order a cheeseburger for dinner. "That's the basics of it."

"And all this time he's been messing with these logger guys?" Amy piped up.

"Not just messing with them," Jack said. "He's been watching them and trying to get someone to pay attention to what's been going on. He's been caring for the animals that have been injured or lost their homes because of the logging."

"So what have you been doing?" Jake asked.

Jack had been helping. He brought Nathan food and swiped medical supplies from his mom's veterinary office. He'd taken care of Nestor – making sure he had food – and brought Nathan medicine when he was sick. He had also been a spy. He listened closely to what people were saying around Smithville and sent letters Nathan had written to officials in the state forestry department, the EPA, and other law enforcement officials. But no one seemed to care. Neither Nathan nor Jack could get anyone to listen to their story about what had been happening in the Smithville State Park. The rangers were on the loggers' payroll, taking bribes to close trails that ran near the valley, and to look the other way when the trucks moved trees away to be sold for hardwood flooring or decks or mantles.

"Why haven't you told anyone at school what you've been up to?" It was the only thing Sam could think to ask. Jack glared at him, an expression of 'you've got to be kidding me' coming through loud and clear. Sam was still a little skeptical. The whole thing sounded a little far-fetched. How could there be an ecological war going on beneath the noses of the residents of Smithville without anyone knowing?

"Because those who do know are either too afraid to do anything or their on the payroll," Jack explained. "There's a lot of money to be made in these woods. Old-growth hardwood is hard to come by these days. And with all the money the loggers are making, it's really no wonder they can afford to buy people's silence."

As quickly as it had been broken, the silence once again filled the cave. Sam wanted to get out of there. He wanted to get back to the trail and on toward home. He felt uncomfortable, like he was sitting in a foreign place and he didn't speak the language. Jack sat on his rock and passed all of them glances, trying to gauge their responses to all they had just learned. He paused for a moment when he got to Sam.

"Do you want to see it? Do you want to see the valley?"

Sam looked at his friends and then nodded silently in affirmation. Of course he wanted to see it. It would be proof of Jack's story. It would be proof that this whole thing was true. "Yes. Yes, I do want to see it," he said.

"Me too," Amy said.

"Me three."

"Me four."

Zach stood up and nodded as if to say 'let's go.' They all stood up. Jack turned to Nathan, who looked a little uneasy, but agreed to go anyway. Nathan didn't like going out during the day. There was a better chance that he would get spotted. He did not want to get spotted.

The loggers called him "The Ghost" because he had managed to wreak havoc on their operation for more than two years without ever being seen. Every time he sabotaged a piece of equipment or left a menacing message, every time he made his presence known, they had sent out a search party. They wanted him out of their hair, away from their operation. They wanted him to leave and never come back. They wanted him dead. But every time they tried, they could never find him. They came close a few times. They got to within feet of where he was hiding, bent down low in the scrub brush or hiding high in the branches of an old oak tree. They came close, but they never got him. It was as if he had the ability to disappear completely. Into thin air. Without a trace. Like a ghost, or some mystical forest creature apparent only to those he chose to be apparent to. Nathan had become a master at leading his would-be killers in the wrong direction, away from where he was, away from the cave, away from Nestor. Once they had searched for three days, coming within a few feet of him, but unable to turn up his presence.

In a sense, Nathan had learned to disappear, to become one with forest around him. He could do this without panic, without thinking. Jack had believed for some time that Nathan had managed to connect with the forest in a way that any outdoors-lover could only dream of. He was a ghost. He was the ghost. And he would never be caught.

Still, Nathan hated to go out during the day. Even a ghost can be spotted during the day. But Jack insisted, and soon all seven of them were making their way through the trees – off the trail, and toward the peak of the hill that looked down into the valley. It was the same peak where Nathan had first seen the destruction the loggers had caused. It was getting late in the afternoon. The sun had already begun to sink in the early spring sky. For the first time since the burlap sack had gone over his head and he had been dragged to the cave high on the hill, Sam thought about his mom. He hoped she was not worried. He hoped she had not gone to Zach's to find him. He hoped she wasn't upset. But Sam's thoughts lasted only a minute or two, because soon they were at the tree line, the place where the hill goes from lush forest to barren rock.

Nathan paused here. Nestor, who had been riding on his forearm, took off and flew up the hill toward what Sam assumed was the valley. They waited for a few minutes, motionless and without saying a word. Amy reached out and grabbed Sam's hand. She squeezed hard and he squeezed back as if to reassure her that everything was going to be okay. Jake and Zach stood on either side of Molly. They all tried not to move. Sam tried to not breath ... not too loudly at least.

After two or three minutes, Nestor returned. He landed silently on Nathan's forearm and put his head down. Then Nathan turned and motioned with a nod that they would continue up the hill. Sam began walking behind the crowd in front of him –

led by Nathan, then Jack, Jake, Molly, Zach and Amy. The thought crossed his mind if only for a moment – had Nestor just gone ahead to make sure that the way was clear? He thought it at first impossible, then subtly marveled at what Nathan had become: a man
able to communicate with animals.

Since they were avoiding the trails, the climb to that point had been difficult, winding between trees and over downed limbs. But once they were above the tree line, the way forward was wide open. It was like being on the surface of the moon – open, expansive and relatively smooth. This part of the hike was like climbing over a bald man's head. Sam was sure he would not have been able to find a trail even if he had wanted to. His breath was quickening and he could hear the others panting. The air was thinner on this part of the hill. But not so bad that they had to worry about serious injury or impairment. A couple of times Sam slipped, the soles of his old sneakers unable to keep in constant grip with the bald rock. He had managed not to fall completely.

As they neared the ridge, Nathan turned and motioned with his hand that they should all get down. Sam (and the others) dropped to their knees, then elbows, and were soon crawling to the top a few feet away. At the ridge, they all spread out so each had a view into the valley below.

The valley looked like a war zone, like a nuclear bomb had gone off, killing everything in its path. Sam looked down and felt numb. The lush forest behind them was like the inside of an empty cereal bowl on the other side of the ridge. Nathan removed some binoculars from his backpack and passed them to Zach, who looked around and then passed them to Jake. Sam tried to take it all in. It was difficult to understand, what lie before him. Everywhere he looked, it was like looking at the result of something horrific. Something inhuman. The stubs of tree trunks that remained looked like his dad's five-o'clock shadow – not covering his entire face, but obscuring it. Down below, Sam could see movement and when Amy handed him the binoculars, he took a closer look.

There were trucks down there, maybe a half-dozen of them. And people moving around, maybe twenty or so of them. Sam focused the binoculars on one of the trucks and could barely make out the letters on its side.

"W-i-l-l-i-a-m-s E-x-c-a-v-a-t-i-n-g" he read, one letter at a time. The distance between him and the trucks made it hard to see. "Williams Excavating?" he said, almost standing up. "Do you guys think?"

Nathan's hand pushed Sam back down to the rock so that he was once again belly-down. Sam passed the binoculars back down the line and looked down silently to the desolate valley. He felt a tear start to well in his eye and quickly brushed it away with his sleeve. The valley seemed foreign. He turned around to look at the tree line below and behind him. He wondered how long it would be until they were gone – until there were no homes left for any of the animals. Growing up in Chicago he had never given much thought to nature, other than the park across the street from their home. Sam was surprised by how attached he felt to these woods, though he had only been in them for less than a day. Nathan, he thought, must be as devastated as the valley.

Sam felt a slight tug on his sleeve. Amy was motioning for him to follow her. The rest of the group had slid down below the ridge and stood up to leave. Sam must have been lost in thought because he had not heard them move. He quickly stood up and started down the rock slope to catch up with his friends.

He had no way of knowing it, but far below on the valley floor someone was watching the hill top. They were watching with binoculars and they had seen Sam's outline as he stood up to catch up to his friends. They had seen him and they were going to come after him. They had spotted him and it made them smile. They smiled an evil smile. An angry smile. A smile that could only mean trouble for Sam.

Sam had no way of knowing, but the loggers now had him in their sights and they would not be happy until they tracked him down and made sure he was not going to talk about what he had seen. Not to anyone. Not at any time.

They would do whatever it took.

Chapter Sixteen

Nathan lead them back down the hill, into the trees and down the path. It was getting late in the day and the spring sun was starting to set – making the woods seem somehow deeper, darker, more forbidding. They had a long hike back and Sam wondered if his mom was already out looking for them. His nose felt open, like an ocean, when he took deep breaths of the cool, damp air. He had forgotten about how much it hurt.

Sam was last in the single-file line of hikers descending the trail. He was behind Amy who turned every now and then to smile at him. He could hear Jake near the front of the line asking Nathan and Jack questions like: "How do they get the logs out without anyone knowing?" and "So Jack brings you food? When was the last time you left the woods? Don't you have a girlfriend somewhere looking for you?"

The ground felt soft, though it had not rained all day. Maybe it was just that they were walking down hill instead of up, or that it was darker. Either way, the walk seemed a little less arduous, but more desperate. Sam had come into the woods to find out the truth, a truth he thought would have to do with a dead boy and a terrible beast. Somehow he wished he had found that truth instead of the one he had. He was prepared for that truth. He was ready to face the consequences. The truth about the loggers and the valley was different, worse. Had they found Jack in search of Craig's body, Sam would have been able to isolate it; he would have been able to think of it as an accident or some kind of mythical misunderstanding that had devastated the life of one of his classmates. But the

logging, the destruction and corruption of what he had seen –
it had shaken his outlook on the world. It is a cruel place.
People can be inherently bad. People can be bought and
some people will do anything for money. The Williams were
probably making a lot of money off the trees they killed. It was
enough even to make the rangers look the other way.
Probably the police too. Nathan knew the truth and Jack
discovered it. He wondered if they felt the way he was feeling
when they both found out. Empty. Shocked. In a stunned state
of awe.

Aside from Jake's incessant questioning near the front, no one
said a word while they were hiking. And the woods seemed
eerily quiet. Sam had chills running down the back of his neck.
Chills that could not be explained by the falling temperature.
He felt a sense of dread, as if something bad were about to
happen. And he was right.

The thud in the center of Sam's back hit him suddenly and at
first he didn't know what it was until he heard a familiar voice.

"Where do you think you're going City Boy?"

Sam stopped dead in his tracks, but could not turn around. He
knew they were back there, the Williams gang. And when the
rest of the group stopped ahead, he knew they weren't alone.
Jake stopped talking and Nathan held his arms out to stop the
group or protect them. Sam looked down the trail and saw a
group of about a dozen strong, haggard looking men standing
in the middle of the trail. He turned and saw that Butch, Bud
and Bart were joined by three other men, all of them carrying
axes or clubs, like short baseball bats. One of the men was

pounding a club into his hand, like he was ready to use it to inflict some damage. Sam tried to put himself between the gang and Amy. He wanted to protect her, but he knew he could not do it all alone.

"It looks as if we have finally found The Ghost," said the man standing in front of Nathan. Nestor let out a shriek that seemed to echo for a year. Sam felt like a gunfighter in the Old West, waiting for the clock to strike noon when both shooters would draw and fire. "You've been causing us a lot of trouble, Ghost. But I think your days of terrorism are over."

"He's not a terrorist! You are!" Molly shouted and the group slowly got closer, Sam and Nathan creating buffers on the ends.

"You're a spirited one aren't you?" The man was wearing sunglasses and a cowboy hat, making it hard to make out his face. "Who are your friends Ghost?"

Butch answered before anyone could say anything. "These are those city kids, pop. And their loser friends."

They were trapped. The trail was blocked. Sam took Amy's hand behind him and held tight. As if on cue, Nestor took off from Nathan's arm and flew directly at the man blocking the trail, using his talons to scratch the man's face. The loggers began throwing stones at Nestor and taking swipes at him with their axes and clubs. Sam and the group used the distraction to run. He held Amy's hand and took off straight down hill, off the trail and into the quickly darkening woods. The rest of the group scattered. Nathan went up hill. Molly, Jake, Zach and

Jack went down hill away from Sam and Amy, and the loggers were confused.

"Get 'em," said the sunglass-wearing man, who was doubled over and trying to fend off Nathan's attacks.

Sam and Amy ran as best as they could, taking big steps and letting gravity pull them down the hill. Sam didn't know where he was going or what he was doing, but he was somehow avoiding the trees that got in his way. It was like a video game. Sam seemed to run without knowing it, holding tight to Amy's hand and weaving his way through the tree trunks and scrub brush.

The gunshot cracked through the air like thunder and hung there for a minute, suspended, then broken by the shrill wail of Nestor's agony. Sam and Amy stopped dead in their tracks. Nestor had sacrificed himself for the safety of them all. Sam wanted to turn back, he wanted to say thank you to this bird he had only just met that day. But the sound of branches breaking up the hill and coming toward them compelled him to move on. It was at this moment that Sam realized, for the first time, that he and Amy were alone. They had no idea where the others were or even where they were going. They only knew that they had to keep going. They had to make it out. They had to find help.

A quick look back up the hill and Sam could see the outlines of five people chasing them. Maybe there were more. Maybe there were many more. Trying to lose his would-be captors, Sam turned sharply to the right and he and Amy began running across the hill, still fighting branches with every step.

His thin wind breaker was tom to shreds and tiny cuts on his arms were beginning to sting from the sweat bleeding into them. Amy had a cut on her cheek that was bleeding and when Sam tried to tend to her she wiped off the blood and motioned for him to keep going.

The sun was gone now and the woods seemed forbidden. After running about 100 yards across the hill, Amy pulled on Sam's hand and they started again down the hill. They were getting tired and felt themselves slow down. A sprained ankle or a broken leg would mean certain trouble from the Williams chasing them. Sam's heart was beating loudly in his chest and his breathing was hard. He had a cramp in his side and the stinging on his arms and ache in his nose made it hard to concentrate. They stopped to listen, to hear even the tiniest clue that they hadn't lost their pursuers, but they heard nothing. No sounds. No twigs. No laughing. Just the sound of their own breath and a breeze moving through the trees.

"I think we lost them," Sam said, bending over with his hands on his knees.

"I wouldn't be too sure," Amy said. She put her hand on Sam's back and did her best to catch her breath. "We should keep going. Find a place to hide out and figure out what we're going to do."

Sam nodded and they began to move down the hill a little more slowly, being very careful to not make any more noise than what was completely necessary. Soon they found a small path. It was not really a trail so much as a portion of the woods that had been beaten down a bit. The walking here was a little bit easier. For one, it was not nearly as steep, but also because there were not so many large rocks to contend with. The moon was bright overhead, allowing light to bleed through the trees in small rays that lit the path well enough. Sam had no idea where they were going. He was not even sure which direction they were going.

They moved along the path cautiously, but still kept a brisk pace. The moon lit the path, but just barely. On either side the light dropped off like a steep cliff. Sam's mind began to wander. He imagined things jumping out from the darkness, dark things, evil things, grabbing them and dragging them off to their doom. Amy squeezed his hand. They were both thinking the same thing. They both feared what they could not see and in these dark woods, there was a lot that they could not see.

Sam was trying to push the images of a savage bear dragging him off by the leg out of his mind when he felt Amy stop behind him, like an anchor bringing a boat to a halt. He turned back to look at her, but she was looking back up the path to where they had just been, beneath the trees in the pitch black.

She pulled him close to her without looking at him. Sam listened hard. His heart was pounding again. His senses were sharp. Then, after a few seconds, he heard it to. Rustling. Leaves crunching under foot. There were no other sounds.

As if on cue, they both turned and ran as fast they could. The path undulated, up and down small ravines where water was gathered making the hard earth into mud. Amy stumbled as they reached the bottom of one of these declines, but Sam steadied her and they kept running. The air was rushing through Sam's ears. He could not hear what ever it was behind them, but he knew it was still there and gaining ground with every step. He tried to run faster and faster, but his legs felt like pudding and were burning. The uneven trail made it hard to set a pace and they jostled with every up and down. Up ahead, Sam could just make out a bend in the path. As they got closer, he jerked Amy's arm and they continued straight, off the trail and down a small but steep slope. They fell onto their butts and slid down to the bottom.

Sam held Amy's head down and rolled over onto his stomach to listen. She looked at him and he placed a finger over his lips, motioning to keep quiet. They were still there, the rustling feet on the trail.

They both tried not to breath, not to move – not to make any sound at all. They were lying there in the dark and listened for the feet to pass them by. As they got closer, Sam realized they were boots. He could not see them from where they were, but he heard them thump and shuffle by, around the bend in the path.

Sam breathed a sigh of relief and whispered to Amy.

"I think they're gone, are you okay?" She looked scared, as scared as Sam felt. He wanted to seem strong for her, like he was not terrified of being in these woods at night, alone, with very bad men hot on their trail.

"I'm fine. I hope everyone else is okay."

Sam had not thought about the others since they scattered. He now worried about his sister and his friends and Jack and Nathan. He hoped they got out and were going to get help. Stay quiet. Stay calm. They're fine, he told himself. They have to be fine. Just stay quiet and keep moving. Get out of these woods. Get out alive and get help. He said none of this aloud, but heard it in his head, like a radio or an iPod playing in his earphones so no one else could hear.

"I'm sure they're going to be fine," he said and they both turned over to lay on their backs. They were lying there in silence and heard nothing, not even a cricket or a frog. They were safe for a moment. They could wait for a few minutes for the loggers to get good and far down the trail and then they would start to move again. They would get out, they would get help and find their friends and Molly. Sam worried about Molly.

Sam's eyes had adjusted to the dark and he could make out the shapes of the trees around them. He could see beyond the black outlines of branches and trunks to the sky above. The stars looked like tiny diamonds. He suddenly wished he were on one of those stars, a million miles away from this place. They were lying there and stared up. They were lying there and caught their breath. They were lying there and pretended to be someplace else. Given any other circumstances, this would have been kind of nice, Sam thought. The quiet. The stars. Amy. It would have been a nice way to spend some time. He wanted to take her on a date. He wanted to play baseball and have her watch from the stands. Maybe he could pitch a good game or hit a home run.

Sam was thinking about all the things he wanted to do when he all of the sudden went blind. The stars disappeared and the trees were gone, like some kind of magic trick. It was white and bright. It stung his eyes and he saw his breath go up in clouds. Amy screamed but Sam could not find the energy or the means to make a sound.

"Well if it isn't our love birds. How's your nose City Boy?"

Butch's voice was like a battle axe shredding Sam's insides and taking his breath away. Butch lowered the flashlight and, though mostly blind from the sudden flood of light, Sam could see he was not alone. There were six of them. Butch, Bud and Bart and three hulking men, bigger than Sam had ever seen in his entire life. One of them stepped forward and grabbed Sam by the collar of his windbreaker, picking him up off the ground. Another grabbed Amy and threw her over his shoulder. They tied bandanas around their mouths and put burlap sacks over their heads. The big man dragged Sam along with his arm wrapped around the boy's head.

This is it, Sam thought. I'm going to die.

Chapter Seventeen

Sam was weak. It felt like he had been dragged for 10 miles. Up and down and over rough terrain. He could hear the loggers grunting and laughing and Butch, Bud and Bart snickering as they carried their trophies back to their lair. Sam tried to yell, but the gag made it hard to breath, let alone talk or shout. Several times he stumbled and every time, he felt himself dragged to his feet again by his head. His neck hurt, his nose hurt and though he was sweating, Sam felt cold. He missed his mom. He missed his dad. He felt himself trying to cry, but his eyes were dry.

What were they going to do to him? Amy? Molly? Where were these men taking them? What would happen when they arrived? All the stories Sam ever heard in Chicago about kids getting kidnapped or killed. All the times his mom told him not sneak out alone. It was all going through Sam's mind and he found himself wishing this was all just a bad dream; that he could just wish his eyes open and he would be back in his room or on vacation with his family. He wanted it to be over and to be safe in his bed where they only thing he had to worry about was homework and baseball tryouts.

Sam began wishing he had never picked up that feather on the bathroom floor. He wished he had never listened to Jake and Zach. He wished he had never moved to this town. He wished he had not fought back when Butch began picking on him. What was he thinking? Fighting back to the bully? He felt silly for wishing these things. But part of him wanted it to be true. Then again, if he had never done those things, he might never had met Amy.

Amy.

What were they doing to Amy?

The ground began to slope down and Sam could feel himself stumbling on almost every step. Still, the big man kept him in the headlock he had held since he picked Sam up off the ground. The descent continued for a long time and Sam had the feeling they were making their way down the valley. They were almost to the logger's camp! Sam tried fighting, but his hands were tied and every time he jerked against it, the logger's grip got tighter and tighter. Sam felt his head getting light and he began seeing spots. The bag on his head felt like it was getting smaller and smaller and he soon began to hyperventilate. He could not control his breath. Short, staccato puffs of air were not enough to fill his lungs and he felt his eyes began to flicker open and closed, quicker and quicker until Sam could not tell when they were open or closed. Then, as dark as the inside of the bag was, everything went black.

Black.

Sam awoke much as he had in the cave the previous day. He was lying on his side, his hands bound. But this time, the gag was still in his mouth and it tasted like sheet metal and dryer lint. His hood had been removed, but it was too dark to see anything. He grew suddenly and painfully aware of every ache and pain that plagued his 13-year-old body. Sam felt like and old man, like he couldn't move if he wanted to.

He took a deep breath through his nose and immediately gagged. He thought he might throw up from the smell. It was awful, like rotten meat and spoiled milk. He kicked his legs to try and roll over and accidentally hit something hard that fell over with a crash. Sam's face touched the floor and it felt like wood, like the dock near his grandmother's lake house, slimy and slick. He heard tick-tick-tick-tick as something small scurried across the floor. A rat? Where was he? Inside a dumpster?

A door opened and Sam's eyes were again scorched by bright light. This time, the light was coming from behind the figure standing in the door in front of Sam. It was light out, really light, like it was the next day. Sam looked around the room while the figure in the doorway stood and surveyed him. He was in a shed of some kind. He had kicked over a garbage can and maggots were crawling across the floor. There were other garbage cans and Sam could see small pellets near their bases. Rat poop. He nearly threw up again.

"It's cozy, I know," said the man, who Sam was starting to be able to make out. He was huge and built like some sort of science fiction robot, as wide in the chest as any man he had ever seen. He was wearing a flannel shirt rolled up over his monstrous arms and a hard hat. His faded jeans seemed to be stretched tightly over his thighs. This was the man, he thought, that had carried Sam through the woods the night before.

"The boss wants to see you and your friends."

He picked Sam up and put him on his feet in one quick movement. Sam felt like a rag doll in this man's huge hands. The man pulled Sam out into the sunlight and onto a dirt road cut into the valley floor. There was a small city of buildings – most of them log cabins. Sam thought he might know where the logs had come from. He was dragged up the road, toward the center of the complex, and once there he looked back to see his accommodations. It was small, maybe six by six and eight or so feet tall with a green roof and a sign over the door that read 'Refuse.'

Sam thought for a second; that seemed like an odd word for a logger to use. Why not just say 'trash' or 'garbage'? But those thoughts were short-lived as Sam was dragged toward a big log cabin with a wrap-around porch and a sign that read 'The Palace.' He was once again scared, once again he feared for his life and those of his friends. He hoped he would find them safe inside or that they had escaped.

The Palace was bigger than any house Sam had ever seen. It was made of logs, like the rest of the buildings scattered throughout the logger village, only it was decorated like a castle. There were huge windows on all three floors and a green aluminum roof. The porch was full of wood furniture – rocking chairs, benches, there was even a swing. The front door was mostly glass, colored glass, painting the picture of a giant snake wrapped around the trunk of an old tree. All of the buildings were standing beneath large trees and Sam couldn't help but see the irony in a logger wanting to live in the woods.

Inside, The Palace looked like some kind of royal hunting lodge. There were animal heads mounted on the walls and a large stone fireplace. The furniture was all made of wood and covered in purple and green fabrics. There was a leather armchair in the corner, next to the fireplace, and sitting in it was an old man with a thin face and gray hair slicked back over his head. He was wearing a suit, a grey suit with a flower on the lapel and he was drinking a cup of tea. He was flanked by two large men that might have been loggers, but they were dressed a little nicer – in khaki pants and checked shirts. The old man watched Sam as he was dragged into the expansive room.

"You must be Sam," the man said, his voice gravely. He smiled, revealing two rows of jagged ochre teeth. "I have been waiting for you."

Sam looked to his left on the other side of the room and saw them sitting on couches: Amy, Molly, Jake and Jack. Nathan was tied to a chair that looked like it might have come from a kitchen table. His head was down and it appeared that he had been beaten. There was dried blood on his face and his shirt was half torn off. Sam jerked toward his friends, but was pulled back by the giant who still had a hold on his bound arms.

"Walt," the man said to Sam's captor, "Please remove the boy's gag and bindings. There's no need to be uncivil."

Walt pulled the gag out of Sam's mouth and untied the ropes around his hands. Sam closed his mouth and swallowed for the first time in hours. His jaw ached and his mouth felt like it had been stuffed with steel wool. Again, he tried to move toward his friends, but Walt grabbed him hard by the arm and led him toward the old man in his leather throne.

"Sam, I do apologize for the conditions of your accommodations last night. But I'm afraid they were the request of my grandson."

Just then Butch came out of a hallway that led toward the back of the house and took his place on the floor at his grandfather's knee.

"I understand you have caused him a lot of trouble at school," the man said. "I hope you do not intend on causing the same trouble here today."

Sam caused Butch trouble? What was this guy talking about? Butch had done nothing but make Sam's life miserable since he came to Smithville. Sam almost protested, but he was too weak and scared to do much other than stare at the old man.

"Now, I hope this nasty business is over and we can move on in a civil manner." Sam put his head down in a sort of half-nod then set his eyes again on the old man. Walt was still holding his arm with a vice-like grip. "Allow me to introduce myself. My name is Bartley Williams and I am your host. This is my home and these men are my family."

Sam didn't say anything. He could barely even think anything.

"I understand that your name is Sam Drake and that you and your sister Molly," Williams looked over Sam to his sister on the couch across the room, "are relatively new to Smithville. I trust that you are enjoying your time in our little burg."

"What do you want from me?" Sam growled.

"My boy, there's no need for such a course tone. Besides what I want is very little. Given your confinement and undoubted worry, I should say that what you want from me is far more important at this particular juncture. "

Sam had no idea what Williams was getting at. He knew what he wanted and that was to get out of here with his friends, alive.

"You see Sam you and your friends, particularly that terrorist over there," he motioned with a limb-like finger to Nathan, "have caused a lot of trouble to our little, err, operation here."

"He's not a terrorist, you are!"

"No. No. No. I will not be spoken to in such a way in my home, not on my property," Williams snapped.

"These woods are not your property," anger welled in Sam. "They belong to the people. This is a state park!"

"Details, details, my boy," Williams was dismissing Sam's outrage, causing him to get more and more angry. "I own these woods and all that is in them. There's no one to say otherwise. Besides, do you think it wise to be disagreeing with me? After all it is I who have shown enough mercy to remove your binding, it is I who have allowed you to live."

"What about Nestor? Where was your mercy when you killed him?" Sam's tone was bit softer, but the edge in his voice remained.

"Who?"

"Nestor. The hawk that you slaughtered along with all the other animals you've killed in order to log this valley."

"Animals? Is that what this is all about?" Williams chuckled at the thought. "My boy, those animals are nothing but beasts and burdens, standing in the way of progress."

"What kind of progress?"

"Why the progress of commerce, my boy." Sam was really starting to hate it when Williams called him that. He looked at Butch and the other men standing around the old man's throne. They were grinning smugly. Butch was smiling ear to ear at the site of Sam's beaten, broken body. "Commerce and economics, two things your friend The Ghost over there does not appreciate.

"For two years, he has interrupted our progress with his terrorism. For two years he had slowed down my family's efforts to reap the riches of this forest. But his time has come and gone. From now on we can continue with our efforts in peace knowing The Ghost will no longer haunt us."

Williams sneered and put his hands together in his lap. His teacup sat on the table next to him. Sam looked back at

Nathan who was teetering on the edge of consciousness and then at Amy, Molly, Jake and Jack. He noticed for the first time that Zach was not with them and Sam immediately thought the worst. Had he made it out? Was he dead in a ditch somewhere? He worried that Zach had fought back too hard and faced a worse fate than what Sam could even imagine.

"Where's Z..." Sam started, still looking at his friends, but Molly shot him the look. It's the look she uses when she wants Sam to shut up immediately. He stopped before mentioning Zach's name, but Williams heard him.

"What's that you say boy?"

"Nothing," Sam uttered and turned back to face Williams.

"It sounded like you had a question. Please, ask me anything."

Sam had to think quickly. He blurted out the first thing that came to his mind. "Where's, err, where do the logs go after you cut down the trees?"

"Well, without getting too specific," Williams seemed delighted by the question, as if his answer would be so brilliant that Sam would marvel at the old man's cleverness. "I can tell you they are shipped to high-paying customers around the world for use in the construction of beautiful log homes like this one."

"Why come to you? Why not buy the logs where they live?" Now Sam was curious.

"Because my boy, these logs, these trees are special. They are an endangered type of hardwood that is illegal to log anywhere else in the world. But I can log them. I can provide them and sell them to the highest bidder."

"But its illegal for a reason!" Sam shouted.

"Yes, because there are only a few places in the world that have them and this is one. Thanks to tree-huggers and terrorists like your Ghost, the market for these trees has been all but closed. But people still want them and there's only one place to get them ... through me."

Williams indeed found himself to be very clever. He was nearly gloating.

"So you get rich and you don't care about anyone or anything else that you might destroy on the way?"

"Rich? My dear boy, I was rich a long time ago. These trees do a lot more than make me rich, they make me very rich and powerful. These trees, this forest, they are gold. Better than gold because you can get gold anywhere, but one can only acquire these trees from me, Williams Excavating."

Sam tried to say something, but Williams dismissed him with a flick of his thin wrist and Walt dragged him to the other side of the room where his friends were sitting.

"Walt, I have grown tired of dealing with these children and the terrorist. I have some business to attend to in the study. If you please, stand guard and keep them quiet while I figure out the next coarse of action."

Walt nodded to Williams, then pulled the bandana and rope that had bound Sam from his pocket and tied his hands together and forced the gag again around his mouth. Williams, Butch and the two guards left the room – and Walt, seeing that they were gone, took a seat on William's throne. He was reading the newspaper and glanced over at Sam, Amy, Molly, Jake, and Jack every few seconds to check on them. They were all bound, all gagged. All of them were helpless. All of them were scared.

Nathan remained unconscious and tied to his chair.

There had to be a way out, Sam thought. They had to get out of this place. They had get help. They had to stop Williams before it was too late and the valley was stripped bare.

Chapter Eighteen

Zach's legs were burning by the time he made it back to the clearing in front of the tree house. The sun was just coming up and his fingers felt cold, but his body was burning. He had been running and falling, staggering and stopping for who knows how long. He hated leaving his friends behind. He hated that they had not made it out with him. And yet there he was, almost back to town, alone and exhausted. He had to keep moving. He had to get help. His friends were depending upon him. He pushed on, up the trail and onto the school property. It was another mile to town and then where?

The police would not be likely to listen to him. After all he was just a kid. And his story was almost beyond belief. He wished his mom and dad were home. Jake lived the farthest away from town. He didn't know where Amy lived. Sam and Molly's house was his best shot. He paused for a moment, no more than two minutes, to catch his breath on the Smithville Square. Standing still felt like trouble, like he was risking his friends' lives. So he pushed on, though he had not caught his breath.

By the time he made it to the Drake's driveway, Zach was all but broken. His body was covered with scrapes and cuts, bruises and mud. He reached the driveway and turned up the gravel, across the front lawn and onto the porch. When he reached the front door, the lights were already on inside. Mr. and Mrs. Drake were awake. And worried.

Sam struggled against the ropes that held his hands together behind his back. He was half-sitting, half-lying on the couch.

He tried to not make any noise that might arouse Walt's suspicion across the room. The ropes were looser than they had been the night before, and he managed to slip one loop down past the heel of his hand. If he struggled enough, he thought he might be able to get free. Amy, Molly and Jake watched him as he shimmied his hands back and forth. And when Sam looked over to Jack, he motioned with his head toward Walt.

Don't get seen, Sam told himself. He pushed himself upright on the couch to conceal his hands behind his back as he continued to struggle against the ropes. A commotion in the other room distracted him for a moment.

"Walt!" someone called. "Come here if you would please."

It was Williams calling for his progeny to join him in the study down the hall. This was Sam's moment, his opportunity. As Walt set his paper aside and got up to heed the patriarch's call, Sam pulled hard against the ropes. His skin burned and he felt a pop in his left wrist that sent shoots of pain up his arm, but his hand was free.

Quickly, he removed the rope and the gag from his mouth, then turned to Amy sitting next to him and set about untying her ropes. Once Amy was free, she went to work on Molly's binds while Sam set Jake and Jack free.

"Hurry, we've got to get out of here," Sam said in an excited whisper. "I can't move," Molly said. "I think I sprained my ankle."

Jake stood up from his seat and took Molly's arm, helping her toward the front door, which was mercifully unlocked and silent in opening. Jack told Sam that he too was hurt. They worked to untie Nathan, then Amy let Jack lean on her as they followed Molly and Jake out the door.

Sam untied Nathan's feet, but he was still largely unconscious. When Sam took the gag out of his mouth, Nathan started to mumble. Not wanting to alert the Williams family to their escape, Sam shoved the gag back into Nathan's mouth and bent down, pulling Nathan by the arms onto his back. The weight of the full-grown man he was carrying and Sam's already exhausted body made it really hard to move. Sam's steps were labored. He was bent over and could not straighten up as he dragged Nathan's nearly lifeless body across the room to the front door.

Outside, the others had made it down the stairs and were shuffling as quickly as they could across the compound toward the dirt access road. Sam stood at the top of the stairs and tried to take a step, but he stumbled and both he and Nathan fell down the hard wooden stairs to the dirt ground below.

"Help!" Sam shouted. "Help me!" He could not lift Nathan from the ground on his own. Jake steadied Molly then ran back toward The Palace to help his friend. They both grabbed one of Nathan's arms and lifted with all their strength. Inside the house, a commotion was stirring.

"They're escaping!" Butch yelled and the sound of boots on the hard wood floor pounded all the way outside.

Sam and Jake moved as fast they could, pulling Nathan toward the road. When they caught up with the others, Sam took Molly's arm and helped her, but the Williams gang was already in hot pursuit.

"Go!" Sam shouted at Amy, who helped Jack move ahead of the rest toward the road. Sam heard the footsteps behind him and let go of Molly just before he felt the impact of Butch's large frame tackling him from behind. Jake tried to help, but Sam told him to take Molly and go. Nathan laid still on the dirt next to Sam, as Butch sat on top of him and grabbed his hair.

"You're not getting away this time City Boy!" Butch said. He turned to his family members, who had been running from the house behind him.

"I got 'em! I got 'em!" Butch yelled, but the men were all standing still as if frozen. "Come on! I got 'em! Get the others!"

Just then a man's voice came over a megaphone. "Let the boy go," he said.

Butch turned back toward the road and saw a dozen police cars parked, the officers out of the cars and leaning on the doors with their guns drawn. He let Sam go and put his hands in the air like the other men in his family.

Sam was too tired to get up. Instead, he just put his head down in dirt and breathed what felt like his first breath in years.

Sam's mom and dad and Zach got out of one of the police cars and ran toward the place where all the kids were standing or lying. Paramedics also came toward them as the police officers moved in. Once the Williams were surrounded, a tall man in a suit stepped forward.

"Bartleby Williams, you and your family are under arrest for kidnapping, reckless endangerment, the illegal transportation of endangered species, trafficking in endangered flora, trespassing and about two dozen other things that you might want to call a lawyer for."

Sam noticed the three park rangers sitting in the back seat of one of the police cars. They must have been arrested on the way in, he thought. Sam's mom hugged Molly and then came toward her son, who was still lying on the ground. She got down on her knees and put her arms around Sam's broken, sore body.

"Oh Sam, I was so worried about you!" She said, tears streaming down her face. "Thank goodness you are alright."

Sam felt safe in her arms. He felt like he had been saved, rescued. He felt like he was at home. Paramedics were attending to Nathan beside him, Jack and Molly. Jake and Zach shared a quick hug and Amy was explaining to police what had happened.

"You have a lot of explaining to do when you get home," Sam's mom said. She was still holding him close, firmly but not hurting him.

"I know mom," Sam said. "I know."

The END

Epilogue

Sam stepped into the batter's box and took a breath. The count was one ball and two strikes in the ninth inning of the game against the Smithville Junior High Woodchuck's rival: the Rileyville Raptors. Smithville was down a run with two outs.

Jack was on second base, having walked and stolen a base. Sam focused his gaze on the pitcher, waiting for the next pitch. When it came, he swung and fouled the ball down the first base line. He stepped out of the batter's box and looked toward the third base coach's box. His dad, who had volunteered to help coach, gave him the sign to swing away and pumped his fist to give his son confidence. When the next pitch came, it was in slow motion. Low and away, just how Sam liked it. He swung and his bat cracked across the field. He had rounded first by the time the ball cleared the centerfield fence.

Sam looked into the stands as he rounded second and nodded to Amy, Molly, Jake, Zach and his mom, who were on their feet cheering loudly. His dad gave him a big high-five as he rounded third and the entire team was waiting for him at home. Jack, who touched the plate just moments before Sam, picked him up and carried him back toward the dugout while crowd cheered and the team went crazy. Sam was the hero. He hit the game-winning home run. He felt like himself again.

It had been a long winter and hard spring in Smithville. But things started looking up after Sam's weekend in the woods.

Bartleby Williams and the rest of his gang were arrested and convicted on fifteen different charges. Bartleby and the older men were all sentenced to fifty years in a federal penitentiary up state. Butch, Bud and Bart were all thrown out of school and sent to a juvenile work center in Nebraska called "Sgt. Wardrip's School for Undisciplined Youth." Sam had not been in touch, be he heard that the Williams boys, who had taken so much pleasure in scaring the life out of countless new kids, dorks, geeks and jocks finally were getting a little taste of what was coming to them. Sam only hoped that they enjoyed lunch time as much as he had on his first day at Smithville Junior High.

As for Nathan, he recovered in the hospital and was released after two weeks. He had thought about returning to his life as an advertising writer, but changed his mind when the State Department of Natural Resources offered him the job as Chief Ranger in the Smithville State Park. He moved into the ranger station and renamed it "Nestor's Lodge." He hired an artist to paint a portrait of the Red Tailed Hawk based on his description and it still, to this day, hangs above the stone fireplace in the station with a small plaque that reads: "Not All Treasure is Gold."

Jack rejoined the world of Smithville Junior High and tried out for the baseball team after some prodding from Sam and his brother. He and Sam have been best friends ever since.

Molly and Zach started going out about 25 seconds after Zach showed up at the logger's camp with the police. In fact, the paramedics were still wrapping up her sprained ankle when she threw her arms around him and planted a giant kiss on his surprised face. Jake claims not to be jealous, but still spends all of his time with the two of them. Just to keep an eye on them, he says.

Sam and Amy spend a lot of time together, mostly talking about anything: from which city has a better chance of putting a team in the World Series – Chicago or Cleveland – to who has a higher score on the Pong machine at the arcade. They both claim to be the winners. She comes to all of his baseball games and he goes to everything she wants him to go to.

They all keep in touch with Nathan. Every Saturday, Sam's mom drives them out to the State Park to help plant saplings in the valley. It's going to take a while, but eventually, Nathan says, it will recover. It will be green again and home to countless birds and animals. It will be around for people to enjoy for years to come.

That's how it is with everything. With a little work and dedication, a little faith and a lot of patience, everything turns out as it should be, as long as we pay attention to the people around us and are careful where we step. You never know what's around the next turn. You never know how things are going to end. Because no matter what you've been told, the truth is always different from the rumors.

But it's always worth so much more.

AN EXCERPT FROM THE UPCOMING SERIES:

Monster Files Case #13
The Grass Man

By Craig J. Heimbuch

Introduction

The cabin had been in Bobby Hamilton's family for three generations. It was a simple building. Made out of logs and designed and built by his grandfather. It had three rooms on the first floor – a kitchen, a bathroom and a living area – and two bedrooms upstairs. One was reserved for Bobby's parents, who took it over after his grandparents got too old for trips out into the woods. The other was an open loft with two sets of bunk beds that looked over the railing and down into the living room below.

Bobby and his family had been going to the cabin for long weekends away and a week every summer his entire life. By the time he got to middle school, the place was like a second home for him and he loved bringing friends up for a weekend to hike in the Appalachian foothills, stomp through the nearby creek or go fishing in the pond down the windy gravel road. But mostly, he liked coming with his family and his dog, a golden retriever named Katie, who had been in the family almost as long as he had.

When he turned 12 last fall, his parents started letting him stay home alone when they went out on dates. At their home, it was no big deal. There were neighbors around and a working phone, plus he had the internet, TV, his Xbox and basically everything he could possibly need. The first couple of times, it had been scary, but he quickly got used to being at home alone – and even looked forward to it. So on this particular trip to the cabin, he felt pretty good about asking his parents if he could stay home instead of going into town for the all-you-can-eat fish dinner held once a month at the Moose Lodge. His parents weren't too sure about it, but over the course of the afternoon, he wore them down. He told them he would be fine, that he wanted to read a book and, besides, he would have Katie to keep him company.

"But there's no phone out here," his mom said. "What will you do if something happens?"

"He'll be okay," his dad answered for him. "We'll only be gone a couple of hours and if he promises not to leave or use the stove, what's the worst that can happen?"

What's the worst that can happen? How many stories have been told that start off with those six simple words? Bobby promised not to use the stove or light a fire, swore he wouldn't leave the clearing in the woods that amounted to a yard and convinced his parents he would just be sitting inside reading his book. Eventually, his mom was convinced and agreed to the plan.

"We will be home at 9:30 sharp," she told him. "Remember what you promised."

"I will," Bobby said. "I promise."

The Hamiltons left their son and his dog, sitting on the front porch of the cabin. He waved to them as they pulled away and looked happy to have the opportunity to prove himself. When they returned at 9:30 sharp, they found a completely different scene. Bobby had locked himself in an upstairs closet and they found him with his arms wrapped around his knees, rocking and crying hysterically. Katie was nowhere to be found. Bobby had held to his promise – neither the stove nor the fireplace had been lit. There was nothing to suggest that he had left the yard.

But something had happened to Bobby Hamilton that night, something that terrified this outgoing boy who had always been eager to talk to anyone. When his parents found him, he was terrified and refused to speak, apart from mumbling the words "grass man, grass man, grass man" over and over to himself as if in a trance.

The Hamiltons called the police, but there was little they could do. There was no evidence a crime had been committed. No sign anyone had tried to break into the house. The dog, they said, must have run away. Other than that, it looked to the officers like a boy got scared being alone in a cabin by himself and the night had played tricks on him. But the Hamiltons knew better. They knew something had happened to their son and that the Grass Man had something to do with it, which is why they called me.

My name is Harrison James and I'm a monster hunter.

One.

Grass Man: File Entry 1

I arrived at the small cabin tucked into the hills and woods of Southeastern Ohio just before sunset, three days after the incident. My clients, the Hamiltons, had returned to their home near Cincinnati a few days before, where I met them for the initial interview. Mrs. Hamilton was the one who got in contact me. Her husband didn't seem to believe in supernatural beings and refused to participate in our conversation. The son, Bobby, was there, though the boy hardly said anything the entire time.

Mrs. Hamilton told me it wasn't like her son to be so withdrawn. He was usually a talkative, polite kid who acted older than his 12 years of age. The boy I witnessed was nothing like that. His appearance was sloppy – his hair was sticking up in every direction, it appeared that he'd been wearing the same clothes for days. His eyes were sunken and dark, most likely because Mrs. Hamilton said he had not slept for more than 10 minutes in a couple of days. He hadn't eaten either. Whatever it was the boy saw, it scared him more than anything he had ever experienced in his life.

Mrs. Hamilton told me about the same story she had on our initial phone call. She and her husband had gone out to dinner, leaving Bobby and the family dog home alone at the cabin for the first time. When they left, everything seemed fine. When they got back two hours later, they found their son in an almost trance-like state in an upstairs closet, muttering the words "grass man" over and over to himself. The dog, a golden retriever named Katie, was nowhere to be found. I was immediately interested in this fact. Golden retrievers are known for their loyalty and, as a breed, don't tend to be the kinds of dogs that run away – especially when they are 10 years old.

The missing dog and the catatonic boy had me interested, but what made me take the case were the words that little Bobby kept saying. Grass. Man. Grassman. Grass Man. Was he frightened by a man named Grass? No, I'd heard talk about a creature known as the Ohio Grass Man before, but I knew very little about it. Was it a human-like creature that appeared to be covered in grass? In five years as a professional monster hunter, I had come across a lot of strange creatures, but I had never met anyone who had first-hand experience with this one – let alone a sighting or an interaction close and scary enough to leave a smart boy in such a state.

There was little I could do from Cincinnati and Mrs. Hamilton agreed to let me stay in the cabin for a week while I conducted my investigation. Her husband, who's family had built the cabin, didn't seem pleased to be letting a stranger take the place over, but I think his wife's insistence and his son's current state left him with little choice.

I packed my gear – the usual essentials for an operation of this type – and drove to the cabin that afternoon. Unlike much of Ohio, which tends to be flat farm land, this corner of the state is wild. The Appalachian mountains begin as foothills here and grow as they head south. The hills, which started small on my drive over, grew larger and more crowded – covered in thick forrest of pine and oak trees that come right to the roadside, making the place feel crowded and claustrophobic.

Doing what I do, I've been in thicker woods with taller trees. I've been in much bigger mountains. I've been in places more remote and isolated that this, but there's something about this place. It's beautiful, but also sad. This place felt like a soul trapped in some sort of cage, wanting to get out.

I inspected the cabin and found it exactly as I was told I would. It was a tidy place, small, but well-built and had the feeling of being loved. The sun was down by the time I had unpacked my gear and I lit a fire in the stone fireplace, turned on a couple of lamps and made my usual field dinner of beans and bacon. I've learned not to live too comfortably when I'm researching a case. There have been many times when I've been on the trail of a monster and had to survive off only what I could scavenge. I've eaten berries and nuts in the Pacific Northwest, survived on shed snakeskin and cactus in the Arizona desert, and caught crawfish with my bear hands in the swamps on Louisiana – that I had to eat raw because all the wood I could find was too wet for a fire. Though there was a full kitchen in the cabin and I was a pretty good chef in my off time, I thought it best to keep my food sparse and bland at this early stage in the project.

Mrs. Hamilton had warned me that there was no internet or phone connection at the cabin. She also said my cellphone wouldn't work in the thick, isolated woods. Not wanting the first night to be a complete waste, I downloaded all the research I could find about the Grass Man before I left and, after I finished my dinner and rinsed out my bowl, sat down next to the fire to learn what I could before beginning my investigation properly the next day.

two.

Grass Man: Background

The first documented sightings of the Ohio Grass Man was in 1978 in the small village of Minerva, about a hundred miles north of the location of the Hamilton's cabin. Two children were playing near a quarry when they spotted a large, hairy creature reeking of rot and decay, roaming among the trash and refuse at the bottom of the open pit. The children ran home to get their grandparents, last name Clayton, who followed the children back to the quarry and verified what they had seen.

Cryptozoology forums on the internet describe a spate of sightings over the next few decades and descriptions vary, but follow a general theme. The Grass Man is described as human-like, walking on two legs and covered in thick, matted hair or fur. Descriptions of size range from just over five feet to nearly ten feet tall and weighing between 300 and 1,000 pounds – which is a big range, but not unusual in the world of monsters and beasts. The most distinctive characteristic of the Grass Man is common to many of the reports: big, almost glowing orange eyes. The eyes seemed prominent in all the reports, whether the sightings happened in the day time or night.

The Grass Man showed up as a note in a lot of Bigfoot forums because of its similar body shape and movement. Not quite a human and not quite an ape. Covered in hair with large feet and hands, walking upright, but not standing up straight. It's thought to hunch over like it has bad posture and has unusually long arms, but not use them for getting around. Many of the reports I managed to find were linked to dogs and deer disappearing or bodies being found mutilated and broken – though many of the commenters on the sites I found believe the Grass Man kills other animals for sport, not food. Interesting stuff.

Many of the forums make reference to ancient tales from the Shawnee Indians who once lived in this corner of the state about 'hairy men' or 'orange eyed' creatures that stalk the night and terrorized small villages or threatened hunting grounds. These reports and legends could not be verified when I was pulling my research together, but are worth a follow-up. I make a note to reach out to my contact at the Native American Museum in Washington for confirmation.

The Grass Man is often described as smelling like rot and garbage and being covered in thick, matted, even greasy hair. But his name comes from his distinct living arrangements. Unlike other Bigfoot-type beasts, the Grass Man does not seem to roam the forest as a hunter and forager. Many people describe finding huts made out of tall grass native to the river valleys of the area. They look like small, grassy igloos and are thought to be the Grass Man's home. In fact, these huts are where the name comes from. Grass does not describe his appearance, smell or habitat, but his home, which makes me wonder: is the Grass Man more domesticated than other creatures? Does he have a family? Does he cultivate food, like early humans? Or is he simply an opportunist who pulls together make-shift dwellings when the need arises? I make a note in my file to investigate further. Perhaps the Grass Man is a hibernator and uses these huts as shelter during the winter months.

And why, if the name describes his dwelling and not his appearance, did Bobby Hamilton mutter the words Grass Man over and over? Had the boy broken his promise to his parents and left the house while they were away? Did he find a hut and make the deduction himself or was there something else to his story?

Little is known about the Grass Man, though there are several similarities to other species I have come across in my research, particularly those related to Eastern Bigfoot. For instance, there are no known incidents of human death related to the Grass Man. Most sightings are from a distance, though there have been reports of the Grass Man appearing to try and bond with small children. He seems to be less friendly toward adults.

Elmer Gantry, a hunter, had a confrontation with the Grass Man in 1983. Gantry was out on an early morning dove hunt in November of that year, when he began to hear strange noises in the woods. An experienced woodsman, he decided to investigate and came across a small clearing where a "giant, hairy creature" appeared hunched over the carcass of a dear. Mr. Gantry raised his gun and started to move toward the beast, no knowing what it was. When he got to within about thirty yards, the creature – believed to be the Grass Man – raised its head and stared directly at Mr. Gantry, according to reports, with large, almost glowing orange eyes. Gantry froze and, before he could fire his weapon, the Grass Man had covered the distance between them in three long leaps and knocked Elmer to the ground. It picked up his gun and threw it into the woods, then knelt over him and leaned in close to sniff the hunter. "It smelled terrible and was huge," he told the local newspaper a few days after the incident. "It sort of sniffed my face and then growled. I closed my eyes, thinking I was about to die, but a second later I opened them and it was gone. The deer was gone. Everything was just gone."

The local police found his shotgun in a tree several days later and Elmer never returned to the woods again.

"It was the Grass Man," he said. "I know it and it was like he warned me to never come near him again. So I don't. Now I just fish."

In 1987, a fisherman named Tommy Finn, was on a trip with several of his college friends. They had rented a cabin not far from where the Hamilton's was located. After a couple long days of fishing and staying up late telling stories around the campfire, one of the men – a local whose name I couldn't find in any of the records – told the group about the Grass Man. Tommy Finn was uncomfortable with the stories and worried his friends would mess with him while he slept, trying to scare him in the middle of the night. It was too late for him to drive back to Pittsburg, where he lived, so he decided the best way to ensure a good night's sleep and protection from his prank-pulling friends would be to sleep in his car. He packed his gear and got in the car, reclining the driver's seat into a make-shift bed. It was a hot summer night and Tommy knew he would not have enough gas to get back into town in the morning if he left the car running with the air conditioning on all night, so he cracked the front windows about an inch and a half and reclined in his seat to sleep with his flashlight laying on the seat next to him.

Tommy had warned his friends before getting in the vehicle that if any of them tried to mess with him while he was sleeping, they may not live until morning to regret it. He thought about his threat when he was awoken at around three in the morning by the sound of heavy breathing just outside his car window.

"I told them to knock it off when I first heard it," Mr. Finn told a police officer the next day. "I told them to leave me alone or I'd run them over. That's when I heard the grunting and pulled out my flashlight."

He flicked the switch and aimed it at the driver's side window expecting to see one of his college buddies or, maybe, a few of them. What met his flashlight's beam instead was a pair of large, unblinking orange eyes.

"I screamed and this thing roared – not like a lion or a tiger, more like King Kong," he said in his report. "I dropped my flashlight and started fumbling for my keys to start the car and I heard the two loud bangs on the roof and the whole car started to rock back and forth like I was in an earthquake. I dropped my keys a couple of times, but eventually got the thing started. I was screaming the whole time and this thing just kept roaring at me until I peeled rubber and got the heck away from that cabin."

Tommy Finn drove around the woods and eventually found his way into a nearby town, where he went to the police station and filed a report. The officer who took his statement asked to see his car. When they inspected the vehicle, there were two dents in the roof in the shape of giant handprints. Tommy laid his own hand in the prints for comparison and the dents were nearly twice as big as his own.

"I think that thing was watching me sleep," he told the officer. "I don't know if I scared it or it scared me, but either way, I went back and there was no sign of the dang thing."

Many of the reported sightings follow a similar pattern. After dark, the creature emerges and is frightened away by interaction with people. When it does appear during the day, it keeps its distance. I make a note to try to find the officer who took Tommy's statement and other people who may have come across the Grass Man or known people who have and then decide to turn in for the evening.

This was shaping up to be one of the most interesting cases I've had yet.

Author's Note

Dear Readers, Parents and Teachers,

In my late twenties, I was working as a newspaper reporter in Southwest Ohio and life was changing at a pace I could hardly understand. I'd gotten married and, before the bouquets wilted (it seemed), had two children. My sisters, who until that time would always be seventeen and fourteen had married and had kids and houses and lives of their own. My college friends had dissipated and scattered across the country and I found myself experiencing long stretches of mental wandering. During my commute, while I waited for my copy to be edited – while pacing around our small apartment rocking our son back to sleep or simply sitting on the couch, in the car or on a bench – my mind would simply tune out the world.

It was during these little mind-cations that I began thinking about the forces in my life that seemed important – family, writing, friendships. Sometimes I would beat myself up for not doing more writing of the style and type that I thought myself capable of. Sometimes I wished I lived closer to my sisters and their families so their kids and ours could be closer. Sometimes I thought about the summers I spent as a kid running around the woods of suburban Cleveland with my friends, making forts and playing capture the flag.

All of these things collided one Saturday night, while I was working the night shift at the paper, waiting for an accident or fire to break the long, quiet monotony of the shift, and I began to write. I didn't know what I was going to write. I didn't have a story in mind. My sister and her family had just moved and I thought about my niece and nephew and their adjustment to a new and unfamiliar life. I thought about moving from Wisconsin to Cleveland as a kid and what it was like to make friends when I was young. I thought about summers spent chasing my cousins around my grandparents' farm in Iowa. And I wrote and wrote for what felt like an eternity, thought it was probably just an hour or so.

A few weeks later, I worked another night shift and decided to write some more. Then again a few weeks after that and again and again until eventually, this small book was written. I printed off copies for my brother and brother-in-law, both of whom were in junior high, and a copy for myself. I saved the master to a CD-ROM and then got busy with life. Years came and went, more kids, more job changes. I wrote other books and told other stories.

Then, in the spring of 2016, I self-published another adventure book called "The Red-Eyed Monster Bass," which I had written over a period of about five weeks with my morning coffee. By instinct or an innate need to complicate myself by commitment, I labeled that book as the first in a series without really knowing what the second book would be. A few weeks later, I remembered this book and went in search of that CD-ROM, only to realize it had been lost in a move. I did, however, have that original hard copy and set about the painstaking task of scanning it, page-by-page, to create an electronic copy. After a few weeks of editing and removing typos, I decided to make it the second book in the Adventure series.

It's been nearly a decade since I starting writing this book and a lot has happened, but I can't help but think of how much remains the same. I still get caught in those wistful fits of memory and fantasy. I still think about family and friends and writing in the quiet moments between work, practices, games and responsibilities. And I still look back to those times in the woods as a kid as some of the most formative of my life.

I could send this book to my agent and try to find a publisher. It might be rejected, it might be accepted, it might be ignored. But I can't help but think that sending it out into the world, directly to you, is the right thing to do. Maybe it will spark some memories of your own.

By not going through a publisher, I run the risk of typos and errors. I don't get the shelf space in a store. I don't have a promotional team. In fact, the only team I have on this is the incredibly talented Troy Hitch, a friend and coworker who dedicates some of his quiet moments to creating covers for these flights of fancy.

And you.

I don't ask much – only that, if you enjoyed this book, you might tell someone who you think might enjoy it as well. If you are so moved, maybe you could give it a review. And if you want to get in touch with me, send me an e-mail at letterstocraig(at)gmail(dot)com. I promise, you're not bugging me and I'd love to hear what you have to say, answer your questions and maybe strike up a relationship.

In the mean time, let me say thank you. If you're reading this, you've probably finished the book. I hope you liked it half as much as I loved writing it. If you didn't, hopefully you're no worse for the wear.

And to the people on whom these characters are based, thank you. Your names are mixed up, your characters are based on little bits of memory I have of you and you probably can't imagine doing any of the things in here – but hey, I'm the author and get to play around a little. I love you, I miss you and I hope you don't mind me dreaming a little dream with you in mind.

All the best,

CJH
April, 2017

Also by Craig J. Heimbuch

For Younger Readers:
"The Red-Eyed Monster Bass (Adventure #1)" (Fieldhurst Books, 2016)

For Adults:
"Chasing Oliver Hazard Perry: Adventures in the Footsteps of the Lucky Commodore who Saved America"

"And Now We Shall Do Manly Things: Discovering Manhood in the Great American Hunt" (Wm. Morrow/HarperCollins, 2012)

"Some People Should Eat Their Young: Travels and Essays" (Fieldhurst Books, 2013)

"Above All Things, Be Useful: Observations and Essays" (Fieldhurst Books, 2013)

About the Author

Craig J. Heimbuch is an award-winning author and journalist, best-selling ghostwriter, husband of one and father of four. He writes stories about adventure and travel, whether through his adult non-fiction or fiction stories for younger readers, and knows no greater joy than setting out for parts unknown with a thirst for discovery and a passion for new experiences. He is the recipient of the Best Non-Fiction Award from the Great Lakes Booksellers Association for his first book, "Chasing Oliver Hazard Perry" as well as several awards for his in-depth and feature writing from his time as a newspaper and magazine writer. "The first book I ever read on purpose was 'Hatchet' by Gary Paulsen," he once said. "I fell in love with how reading can take you to places no other experience can." He's been described as "exactly what American travel writing needs" by former Esquire editor Will Blythe and Publisher's Weekly described his writing as "Sometimes funny, sometimes bittersweet, and always well-paced adventures." His newest work, The Adventure Series, are character-driven adventure books for younger readers (8-13) in the spirit of Gary Paulsen and Goosebumps.

50067337R00095

Made in the USA
Columbia, SC
02 February 2019